LYING PERFECTLY STILL

LAURA FISH

First published 24th October 2024 by Fly on the Wall Press
Published in the U.K by
Fly on the Wall Press
56 High Lea Rd
New Mills
Derbyshire
SK22 3DP

www.flyonthewallpress.co.uk
ISBN: 9781915789228
EBook: 9781915789235
Copyright Laura Fish © 2024

A CIP Catalogue record for this book is available from the British Library.

To all children living with HIV and AIDS.

With love and gratitude to those of you who helped with writing this book — whether known or unknown, your generosity is woven through the storyline and imprinted on these pages.

"If you have come here to help me, you are wasting your time. But if you have come because your liberation is bound up with mine, then let us work together."

-    Indigenous Australian woman cited in "The Manilla Declaration on People's Participation and Sustainable Development" 1985

PART ONE

PROLOGUE

She slides the glass door open and steps onto the bathmat. She was born two months and twenty-two years ago. According to her horoscope, her quests for freedom and adventure are typical for her age. She grabs a towel, pats goosepimples dry. Black curls rest stole-like around her shoulders. The wiry mane gathered into one bunch; she turns. The mirror captures her plump cheeks; the broad nose she dislikes.

A line of gold glints around her neck. She toys with the fine chain bequeathed by her mother. Everything at the cottage soured when the cancer spread and took her mother's life. At sixteen, Koliwe's heart had shattered into icy shards. Then she went straight from washing up at the pub each night to Andrew's bed at the neighbouring farm and found refuge wrapped within his quietly spoken white limbs.

The nightdress beneath her feet is damp from the shower's spray. She forgot to bring clean clothes from her bedroom. Naked, she tiptoes along the landing. Moses' door opens. He wears his blue velvet dressing gown and is blowing his nose into his fingers. Father and daughter are face to face. Disgusted, Koliwe shrinks from him. Her right arm shoots across her breasts, her left hand cradles the triangle of hair beneath her belly.

Confronted by a naked daughter – what to feel? Where to look? Parts of her pear-shaped body he has not seen since she was about ten. She knows that scowl – the crow's feet splaying towards his temples; lines scoured either side of his lips; each tuck and pucker the texture and colour of a wrinkled prune. Moses glares at his daughter. She stumbles backwards until her buttocks brush the banister spindles. Moses shuffles backwards too. His breath reeks of last night's whiskey. His eyes divert to the tears of water dripping to the carpet from her hair.

She streaks to her bedroom faster than a hare to a burrow. Slams her door shut, slings on underwear, T-shirt; jiggles into jeans.

The springs squeak when she clambers onto the bed. Cupping her chin in both hands, she traces the blanket's detailed pattern spun by single threads. Threads entwine, brown blending with red as a tapestry spreads in folds and furrows, lying like the hills and hollows of the countryside woven into her life. She cannot bring Andrew back to the cottage. Because of her father. Wiping the wetness streaking her cheeks, she swallows the desire to flee. Her aim to help feed the world is naïve at best. Leaving England means breaking with Andrew. Yet the dream to escape, to find a new life, churns and grows, and cannot be supressed.

She rummages through drawers. Searching for what? Love is not stored here. Her mother's two-tone Chanel dress is wound around photographs taken at her parents' London wedding.

The first Christmas without her mother had all the wrappings with nothing inside.

"Why do you hate me?" her father had asked.

"I don't hate you."

Koliwe's feelings for him were frozen. *I feel iciness*, she had replied to herself.

She has waited for years for the thaw. Their jealously guarded grief is kept separate from each other. She disentangles the dress, crushes its softness against her cheek. Takes comfort in the black and white print; the lingering odour of sixties glamour. As a small girl, she had marvelled at her mother's body. The fluidity and peculiar curves held an innocence – the pale gleam of magnolia petals in spring. Beside the banister post she pauses. Each year as the months wore on, her pink mother bronzed. They used to sit on the riverbank fanning their faces languidly with one hand, cool as the English countryside in the height of summer.

The kitchen flagstones are cold. Last night's fire is dead. After that unspeakable encounter, she cannot eat breakfast with her father. Her flesh still tingles from shock. She switches on the radio. Opens windows to let in the morning chorus. The chill rush of dawn air is sweet with a meadow-flower scent; the sky is lightening to coral-pink.

Out she slips onto a path flanked by cow parsley and waist-high nettles. By the time Moses has stomped downstairs, switched off the radio, slammed the windows shut, she is scampering from the cottage like a crab from a breaking wave.

She presses her fingertips to her temples. Worry kept her awake all night. She is cloaked in wretchedness. She should have worn a coat. Everything is clenched.

She fast walks the circular route down the valley and up the hill, her ears deaf to the bull calf bellowing for his mother. Twenty minutes later she is panting up the garden path.

Bursting through the kitchen door, she yells, "Dad!"

Tobacco smoke wreathes its way through the low-ceilinged cottage. The study door is ajar. Her father is in a foul mood, collapsed in his armchair, reading the bible aloud with religious fervour. Her heart sinks. She creeps upstairs, flops onto her bed. Does she belong with this bitter, chaotic man? How her mother loved him goes beyond understanding.

When the grandfather clock strikes eleven, she grabs the car keys from their saucer and drives into town. The blue sky is painted with puffy clouds by the time she strolls to the farm to drop off the weekly groceries.

"I've got your shopping," Koliwe sings from the doorway.

Nutshells splinter under her sandals as she ducks beneath a basket of pansies dangling from a chain above the doorstep.

Len stands with his back to her; flies circle his balding head. The kitchen buzzes with blue-bottles; bunches of herbs and cornflowers hang drying from the ceiling.

"You alright?" Koliwe asks.

Len turns from packing his pipe. "Hello, little dove. I suppose so, yes."

She gives him her quizzical look. Frequently she finds herself captivated by what, as a child, seemed unexceptional, like the creases in Len's weathered cheeks, the weariness in his liquid brown eyes. An odd surge of affection for him surfaces.

"Joyce," Len calls, "Koliwe's here."

The farmer's wife, a reedy, straight-speaking woman emerging from the cool darkness of the pantry, is graced with little tenderness. She nods, then cocks her head of silvered grey hair at the crushed hazelnut shells. "Squirrels 'ave been busy," she says.

Involuntarily, Koliwe jolts from a movement within.

"What's the matter, your father's health?" Joyce takes up the grocery bag slumped in the doorway.

Koliwe stiffens with pride. "No, it's nothing." Saying goodbye, she shakes her head, but her throat thickens and aches.

Her slight shape turns, disappearing in a flash through the gates. It is the end of summer. Swallows dive-bomb from the farmhouse eaves, warning her, then swoop across the cobbled yard and out over rows of newly cut hay.

Koliwe takes the bridle path where bindweed flowers beside the river. If she squeezes the base of the white buds, drawn in for the close of day, they pop up and out. *Granny-pop-out-of-bed*, her mother used to say. She reaches a leafy hollow. Here, the river's sheen flickers muddy-bronze and mercury, marbling tree trunks with shimmering light. Koliwe's thoughts are leaves prancing on the breeze. Farm labour pays Andrew's rent. Can she be content with his condescending scent of over-ripe apples and matured sweat; brown hair flopping over his forehead? Can she love this man who gives her reassurance when she clasps her body to his, then lets go, her finger-marks dissolving like snow on warm skin? How to construct a different self? She scrambles up the bank. Leave home? When reaching the deep tractor ruts leading to the cottage, shrill tones pierce the air. She dashes through the kitchen to the study. The phone stops ringing. The grandfather clock is struck dumb and wants winding.

Where is her father? His drinking seeps into everything.

Sunlight streaks the faded cloth of her father's armchair, a chest of drawers, six scarlet and turquoise Russian dolls, a jewellery box filled with childhood pleasures she once loved to idle through. Beneath the box is his sketchbook. His paintings adorn the walls – a warrior in leopard skins melting into blue-green flora; a woman's dark and delicate face wrapped in tortoiseshell cloth, the aunt she longs to meet – conjure a dream-like quality. Etchings on a copper plate bring to life the relentless flow of the river. The feeling of turbulence. The rush and transparency. What seems important pales to insignificance in the chase of the river – the sparkle of black and white – the craft of the etcher, letting the light through. There is comfort in the familiarity, yet something is wrong. Her sight wanders to his sketch of a little girl peeping from beneath a floppy sunhat. Crosshatching creates shadow on the daisy-patterned frock. The veil of time lifts. He has caught the aloof expression she had as a child. By the mirror she pauses, peers into her restless eyes. Torn between opposing forces – her dark-skinned father. Her mother, white. Belonging to two worlds and yet to none.

"Dad?" she shouts. She climbs the rickety stairs, searches rooms silent and empty. How his swarthy face, lined and toughened with time, grimaces at even the briefest mention of Swaziland – the country he renounces as godforsaken and dangerous.

But she is curious about her ancestry. One day she had asked, "Could you take me?"

"You want too much," he had snapped, wrinkling his brow.

Hating the father she loves comes as a shock. Neither understands the other. The daily clashes are agony. Both are imprisoned in separate cages of pain. Deaf to what the other says. Paralysed by emotional wounds. Blind to new ways of behaving.

She scuffles downstairs, wreathed in the fusty smell of whisky and oils on canvas. Tell-tale signs clutter the circular rosewood table: another empty bottle, an ashtray overflowing with cigarette ends. She stumbles across the bible left open on the carpet. Leviticus 18:6-19: *None of you shall approach any blood relative of his to uncover nakedness; I am the LORD.* The sun's sharp perfection creeps across the contours of her anxious face. Where is her father this time?

Outside, on the overgrown path, she shivers with fury and love. Uncertainty hangs in the air, mingling with a sense of loss. She trips over tractor ruts. Startled sheep scatter. Rain freckles her forehead as she sprints towards the bridle path far below, hemming the river – a rumpled, reflective sheet, flowing beneath the bridge's arches. Halfway down the hillside, the view across the valley opens out. Deep in the English countryside, the changes that come with time have stopped. The scene has the faded look of a Constable painting, still and misted. There are the tall chimneystacks of the grey slate farmhouse, the tumbledown barn, furrows where the manor once stood, hedgerows enfolding twists of road. She runs past the creamy-white cow, swishing its tail around a sucking calf, along the wooded path and towards the thick, green river.

She stares in disbelief at the figure balanced on the high wall of the road bridge. His arms raised to shoulder height; hands outstretched. Given the amount he usually drinks, how has he achieved such a feat, climbed that high? He edges across mossy stones. He cannot swim. Her heart is a clasped fist. Does he realise what he is doing? The pendulum of time stops swinging. Moses' body, a T shape, shifts to the highest arch above the river. His drunken legs buckle. The bridge is a heartbeat away.

She screams and like a stone dropped from a wall Moses falls all the way down, to the river.

She is bounding between trees in short bursts of explosive speed. Down the grassy slope, between tall bulrushes dappled with sunlight, dashed with shade. Down the bank through thick and silent air. She reaches the pebbly strip of beach, scans the murky depths where the bridge's middle arch slices the water's flowing skin. Here the river is broader, deeper. Where is the splashing, the gasping, the thrashing? Where *is* he?

She slips sandals from her feet, wades into the icy flow. Ducks dart skyward in a quacking whir of wings. The mottled riverbed glistens crimson and mustard-yellow through disturbed silt. Her stomach tightens; red waves of emotion build. Time is passing. She wades until waist deep, thrusts forwards from the bank with as much force as she can, launching into an extended glide then panicked breaststroke. Swirling water buffets her chin. Foam circles twirl across the river's thick green face, coagulating in the middle, swelling downriver into a turbulent white gush. There is an ominous absence of light where Moses' body bobs beneath the bridge's shadow. Koliwe's arms are sculling. Her feet flutter to tread water, stirring memories of his final painting. The artist submerged in the river, professing his own death. The most troubled face she has ever seen.

Screened by spear-like reeds, his forehead surfaces, the skin varnished with water. She swims against the current. Chin angled upwards, his body rises, eyes drained of life. She reaches out; her fingers brush his chest. The chain of his silver crucifix hooks around her wrist and snaps. She reaches out again. The whale-like mass is too heavy. Already the current's force drags her deeper, will pull her to the depths. There is the thump-thud-thud of her pulse in her ears, the gurgling, gulping river, a giddy sickness of guilt and grief.

She scours the river's course to the curve downstream, one fist clutching her father's broken silver chain. Close by, his striped shirt balloons, then deflates and recedes from sight. As his face rises one last time, she reaches for his collar, grabs at his nose. Her heart flutters with determination. But the sodden mass sinks. As swiftly as he appeared, water washes back over. Unbearably, he vanishes. He is gone.

CHAPTER ONE

Mbabane's pavements swarm with fast-moving hawkers. Stalls sell watermelons, dusky-pink guava; the air is close, hot and scented bittersweet with marula fruit. Amongst street beggars gathered in the plaza is a girl, aged no more than thirteen, in high heels and a ragged indigo dress. She has a wide forehead, a delicate jawline, a neat pear-shaped nose. Car brakes screech as she totters across the road, a child's doll wedged beneath one arm, a six-pack of beer balanced on her head. Koliwe feels unstable. There is something disconcerting about an adolescent girl in an older woman's clothes.

Koliwe remembers at a similar age she was the contradiction: the one drop of colour on a white canvas. She knew of Swaziland only from the few traditional tales she heard when settled upon her father's knee. "Don't ever go to Swaziland," he once told her. "They'll eat you alive." He cut himself from his country. He had been so proud. But he was damaged by the loss.

Here, amidst mansions, iron shacks and match-box houses, his loss has become her burden. Crossing tarmac dusty and red, she is an invisible other. Then the market's cheerful energy smacks her in the face – a pot of cultures, racy colours, the bustle of bargain-hunters; the reek of rubbish, stale urine, decomposing dreams.

Since leaving Oxfordshire she's seen nothing of the culture she expected. Who created this confusion and mess? The men are not dressed like the warriors in her father's paintings, with animal pelts over red loincloths; neither do they carry ox-hide shields, sturdy knobkerries, or feathers in their hair. Cars taxi along the main road. Boys smoke on every street corner, disillusionment in their eyes. Unlike images on the TV news, here their stares cannot be switched off.

She is now in the back of a taxi on the driveway to Colonel Johnston's house, sweeping away from central Mbabane between colourful flower beds and sleek green lawns. Electric gates stand sentinel before the gatehouse. A line of taxis waits at a rank. The gates swing open effortlessly, revealing more lavish gardens and another set of gates. The Johnstons' impressive three-storey house with wooden shuttered windows stands on the far side. Roses climb the white-washed walls. The drive meanders round the croquet lawn and a shimmering turquoise swimming pool.

Stout, crimson-faced, Colonel Johnston, in a black dinner jacket with polished brass buttons, is stationed between two bay trees; wispy strands of whitish hair stripe his shiny pate. Like the earthenware pots either side of the doorway, he looks too heavy to move.

He raises a glass of sherry. "You must be... er, the new girl Cameron Cuthbert said was joining the fold."

"Yes, I'm Koliwe." She glances at the invitation card's italicised font. She is just a blur mounting the steps of the wide verandah to his home.

"Come, meet my wife." His hand furtively strokes the smooth olive skin on her shoulder.

Human contact has been scarce in the six months since her father drowned, and the shock of the old man's touch sucks away her breath. The colonel guides her to a roomy kitchen. The floor is tiled black and white in the stark contrast of a chessboard.

"Darling, meet... er..."

"Koliwe." She tilts up her chin defiantly.

The colonel's wife is quite the opposite of him. In an orange and brown floral-print chiffon dress, she darts around freestanding units and worktops cluttered with sharp knives and electrical appliances. She has brought out as much of England as she could carry; so much, in fact, the Swazi staff, in their lace-up shoes, beige tunics and mop caps, look like foreigners in their own country.

"You're African?" Mrs Johnston glances at Koliwe, slicing carrots urgently.

"English, actually."

"African," announces the colonel abruptly, "so am I." Yet he, too, speaks with a British accent.

Venetian blinds screen the glass door to the back yard. Koliwe squints between the slats to flittering duets of butterflies before a corrugated iron shack. A maid washes clothes in a metal bowl. Her dress is threadbare; strings of glass beads hang into the grey water. Palm tree fronds bow and beckon, casting afternoon shadows over her back.

A rash of liver spots pattern Mrs Johnston's wrinkled face, her thinning, lavender-blue hair is piled high in a nest on top of her head. She examines the canapés. "We don't see God's creatures in terms of black and white. We simply see God's creatures," she says primly, garnishing prawns with lemon and parsley. "Blackie!" she shrieks. "Get out!"

Koliwe jumps, as a Labrador slinks around the kitchen door. Blackie is undeniably black. A nervous friction moves in the air.

"Where in the world has my new blender gone?" Mrs Johnston wheels round, her sequin-blue eyes searching the sideboards. Mountains of crockery are stacked on the drainer. The dishwasher wants emptying. She digs out the liquidiser, then presses lemons into it, squinting in the direction of the pantry while the mechanism moans at full speed.

Another maid emerges from the pantry and places a jar of pickled gherkins amidst a pile of potato peelings. Koliwe presses back against the wall, out of the way.

"I just hope the guests don't arrive all together." Mrs Johnston flusters around the maid, mixing olive oil with balsamic vinegar.

Blackie is back again.

"Don't pester me for food bits, I'm trying to cook," Mrs Johnston says, looking sternly into the dog's beseeching eyes.

The colonel trips whimsically around the kitchen. "Anything I can do to help?"

"Do let the poor girl know who else will be coming," whispers Mrs Johnston. Her hips barrel from side to side and her bosom – two flamingo-pink blancmanges – wobbles in her low-cut dress, as she bends to kiss Blackie's wet nose.

Following his wife's instructions, the colonel turns to Koliwe, "There's… er, an expat couple, they're from England, or Africa, or wherever." He glances at his gold wristwatch. "They really should be here."

His wife yells at Koliwe over the dishwasher's roar, "You'll probably know them, my dear."

The doorbell rings. The guests *have* arrived altogether. First are two Americans and a British-German couple. Mrs Johnston's expression is animated when she performs the introductions, while the colonel tops up his own glass and downs it in one. Despondency knots in Koliwe's stomach as more women flock in, all talking theatrically in paisley frocks and shimmering, gossiping waves of satin.

"You're here with your husband?" asks a wide-girthed woman with jade-green eyes and a chestnut-brown bob.

"No," Koliwe replies, "I'm with U.K Aid."

"Koliwe's new, aren't you, my dear?" Mrs Johnston swivels Koliwe round to a solid square figure with a ready smile. "Koliwe, meet Jeanette."

"Yaar." Jeanette's rouged and powdered cheeks give her face the crusty appearance of parched, cracked mud.

"Jeanette has recently taken up horse riding," Mrs Johnston chats on.

"The dressage horse died of a heart attack," Jeanette says. "It was attacked by a swarm of bees." Jeanette observes Koliwe as though she is a tropical fish in a display case. "Why did you come to Mbabane? You're running from a man?"

Quietly Koliwe replies, "I just wanted a fresh start."

A man in a jazzy red shirt slides into their conversation.

"Jeanette's husband, Martin," Mrs Johnston announces.

Pressing her lips together, Koliwe half-smiles at him.

Martin's eyes swim with a lively enthusiasm; his hair is mousy-brown; skin a raw beef colour. Koliwe tries to think of something clever to say.

"We adore dinghy sailing," Martin tells her. Armed with good looks, he snatches glasses of wine from a silver tray, offers them around. He rocks back and forth like a metronome as he talks on, "Last summer we raced in the Cowes regatta. We capsized a few times but that wasn't a big problem and we soon set sail again, hey." He slips his arm around Jeanette. She steps aside. Both drink at a rate of knots.

Mrs Johnston introduces Koliwe. "Meet John and Clotilda. Clotilda was born in Zimbabwe and is the country's leading dermatologist. John went to Zimbabwe to study malaria, met Clotilda, and stayed. He's now an authority on diseases. As it happens, there's a plague of malarial mosquitoes sweeping through eastern Zimbabwe at the moment, so there will be a lot to talk about!" Mrs Johnston stops in full flow and rushes to the kitchen.

Beyond Clotilda and John is a view of Blackie at the far end of the house on his hind legs, front paws resting on the sideboard, wolfing down carefully prepared canapés. Mrs Johnston flies at her dog, whooping.

A maid emerges from the back doorway. Koliwe swipes a glass of spumante from the silver tray. The skin around the maid's nose wrinkles from squinting, her eyes dissect Koliwe. Koliwe can tell the maid cannot quite place her. The colonel ushers Koliwe into the study.

The study, smelling of sour cigar smoke, is broodingly dark and musty.

"You'll adore our collection of paintings," the colonel declares.

The past – a shadowy, spectral presence – is both visible and invisible in the leather chaise longue with scuffed edges, the cushions moulded into the sagging brocade backs of armchairs. Ornate gold lettering gilds the stolid spines of the books lining walls from floor to ceiling.

Generations of the Johnston family's eyes follow her with intently, as she passes gold-framed portraits of rectangular faces, narrow noses.

"Dinner will be a feast. Prawns from Mozambique, fillet steaks and halibut with a hollandaise sauce." The colonel uncorks bottles, raising his greying bushy eyebrows, pursing his lips. "The vegetables were grown in the gardens. The wine's a nineteen-seventy-four vintage. I've given the best years of my life to these people; I expect something in return." The colonel glances at Koliwe and cocks an eyebrow suggestively. His hand wanders once more to her shoulder. "You coloured girls are so damnably pretty."

She goes cold, livid, blue, backs into a Chesterfield sofa, then retreats towards a cabinet with shelves displaying Swazi artefacts – stone and wood carvings, exquisite beaded necklaces, decorative amulets.

The colonel lights a cigar. Smoke curls a grey serpent around his freckled forehead. Koliwe's wintry disgust is keen. But it is only six o'clock, too early to leave.

Outside, the sun, a scarlet fury, is setting the sky on fire. Koliwe stares stonily at a collection of prints on the dowdy wallpaper: an elephant herd charging through orange dust plumes; portraits of a Mediterranean-looking girl and boy with sentimental expressions and dewy eyes. Great glassy tears roll down their rosy cheeks.

The last slits of amber light sinking below the horizon fill with memories. The views over the misted valley. The oaks in the copse running down the hillside. Leaves cloaked in autumnal rust. The farmhouse chimneys silhouetted against a hazy sky upon which smoke curls. The rhododendron garden sloping to the river. Her glowing excitement at frost-covered hills. Falling snow could not be heard, just the hush when flakes had settled; the creak of branches under their blanket; the flurry of flakes at the windowpane muted by wind on a blustery day, rising above the river's constancy. She found peace when immersed in countryside. But the memories blur when she thinks of her father. Anger and pain were rocks he carried.

Her palms are sweating; a blister throbs behind her sandal straps. The elaborate card announcing the Johnstons' annual dinner party had come as a pleasant surprise, though how or why it arrived is mysterious. Does she bring fresh blood to the expat community? Had the Johnstons connections with U.K Aid?

The colonel's head pokes around the doorway. "Sherry?"

"Still here?" asks Jeanette, who sails in after him.

"When did British aid workers first come to Swaziland?" Koliwe enquires, curious.

Jeanette's smile drops from her face; probing was unexpected. "Who?"

"The missionaries," the colonel bluntly states. "Used to come for God, now they come for money. Couldn't get a job in the United Kingdom – or even in the Kingdom of God – if they wanted to. Standard of life's better in the Kingdom of Swaziland, too."

Mrs Johnston bears a salver of canapés. "Are you getting out enough, dear?" she asks, as though Koliwe is an elderly aunt of whom she has charge. "You know there's a cinema, then there's the theatre."

"Hardly call it that," grunts the colonel. "Did you hear about their last production? Terribly funny. Aileen was on the book. Jenny leapt on stage, leotard back to front, exposed her boobs for all to see. Then—"

"We've heard the productions are surprisingly good," his wife interrupts, with her genteel intonation. The final rays of sunset spread a pomegranate pink blush across her face.

The study is now smoky and charged with chatter. Wandering from one clump of guests to the next, Koliwe is poised on the edge of a cliff top, with the crowd behind wanting to push her into the wrathful waves below.

"Koliwe Dlamini," says a tall man, who has stepped in front of her.

They have not met since her interview at U.K Aid's London office, and a flush rises to her cheeks.

"Koh-lee-way. That's how you pronounce your name," Cameron says, more as a statement than a question. He possesses a suave manner; the burr of his Scottish accent, the trilling of the r, makes his diction distinctive, as though words are trapped in the back of his mouth. The blue-grey eyes peer at her through the wavy brown and silver-streaked fringe.

Koliwe is relieved by his courtesy and firm handshake. "Am I glad to see you again."

"And I'm glad you received this evening's invite," he says. "I made sure you were on the list. Welcome to Swaziland's expat colony." He gestures around the room, his athletic build shielding her from the party. He stands his ground as squarely as a hyena – powerful jaw, thick neck, broad sloping shoulders. "You're looking forward to starting on Monday?"

"Yes. I arrived a couple of days early, to settle in."

The maid flits past with more canapés. Sipping sparkling wine, slightly queasy, Koliwe regrets taking two crab canapés. Whenever she takes a mouthful, she feels flecks of meat stick to her cheek.

Cameron's hand brushes stray ringlets from the side of her face.

"Can I help?" He has pulled a tissue from his pocket and is holding it out for her. With his sad blue-grey eyes and assured demeanour he is, in a way, attractive. "Whatever you do, don't go out walking in the countryside alone," he says. "Things might look harmless, but you never know what's lurking round the corner."

She is back on the plane, sliding the *Swazi Times* from the string pocket attached to the seat back, hovering over murder stories on the front page. Shootings, rapes of women and children. Violence crept like an inky stain from each page.

As if on cue, thunder rumbles dramatically and lightning flashes on and off above the mountain ranges. Cameron shrinks against a wall. Never has she seen terror so quickly change a man's face.

"I've a deathly fear of lightning," he says. "You've found me out." He frisks his jacket for a cigarette. His fingers tremble as he lights the tip; the backs of his hands are streaked with veins. "There are more lightning-related fatalities here than anywhere else. The first time I saw someone struck, it made an impression. I was only twelve." He reaches for his drink, and steps towards her as the thunder abates. "We'll have to get together," he says, tossing back the liquid in his glass, giving a hardened grin. "I'm used to this place. Locals know me. I speak siSwati, of course. With a name like Koliwe Dlamini, I take it you do too."

"Actually, I don't." Koliwe hopes he hasn't detected embarrassment in her voice. "Do you live in town?" she asks quickly.

"My home's Mbabane, but I also have a hunting lodge in the mountains."

She says they must talk again and excuses herself for the ladies' room.

Dust shimmers on the looking glass; a young woman stares out. Half her face shiny with makeup, the other half distant and dark. The girl she strived to be has vanished. She tucks curls behind her ears, straightens the Chanel dress. The reflection twists, turns. Neat, sophisticated – the perfect impression. She liked the way Cameron was interested in her. She accentuates the lines of her eyes, brushes eyelashes with mascara, paints lips crimson. Vignettes from their first meeting filter into her thoughts like the slits of afternoon sun that had strobed him as he moved.

The whine of a barrel organ drifted through the traffic, up the steps and into the entrance hall of the shabby London Edwardian townhouse with its winding staircase, flaking paint. She found it hard not to reflect upon previous job interviews that had fallen through, even harder to hope. Suspended in a mirror on the third-floor landing, an aspect of herself she had not seen before hovered between confidence and fear. Calm one moment. Anxious the next. Naïve pouty mouth; brown eyes framed by ringlets, haunted by a past she wants to forget.

The receptionist, an ambitious graduate no older than herself, with hair scraped from her sharp face into a ponytail, glanced up from the desk. "Mr Cuthbert is waiting for you," she said in honeyed tones. "U.K Aid's on the top floor."

Koliwe continued upstairs as though stepping on thin ice.

Cameron's office was rustic, minimalist: a woven mat, wood flooring, executive desk, designer chair. He had a thin face of simplicity and strength, thick grey-brown hair. He stood up, adjusted his black tie; a red HIV ribbon was pinned to the lapel of his seal-grey suit.

"Koliwe Dlamini? *Miss* Dlamini?" he asked.

"Yes."

"Call me Cameron." He gestured for her to take a chair. Clearing his desk of files, setting aside the nameplate that read: *Cameron Cuthbert, Project Coordinator,* he assumed a thoughtful expression and sat down, rearranging papers. A busy man on his way up the ladder. His tone was formal and low, "I must apologise on Mr Callow's behalf. Mr Callow's head of our Southern Africa branch. He can't be here today. He is meeting new recruits upon their arrival in Swaziland."

His arched eyebrows raised in anxious expectation, his sight flitted across her interview clothes – an apricot-coloured linen jacket, matching pencil skirt and a flame-coloured scarf looped loosely around her neck – eyes, darker than her chestnut-brown skin. She slid her wiry limbs onto the chair, hitching down the close-fitting skirt, trying to hide her knees.

Strips of light, soft as burnt sienna, the slant of the sun through the blinds, caught his cheek with a tinge of amber and livened the glow to his skin. "You're just twenty-three?" he asked. "Tell me about yourself."

Nervousness crept up her spine and out through her words. "I know there'll be challenges." She shunted her chair closer to his desk. "I don't want to be kept in a protective bubble…"

Cameron nodded encouragement. "You're flexible? Determined?"

Her face stiffened and grew suspiciously solemn. "Oh, I'm good at teamwork, and I was popular at university and in school." This was not entirely true.

"The contract is for one year." He uncovered a map on his desk and pointed out southern Africa. Sliding his finger around it in a full circle, he homed in on Swaziland.

Koliwe's one wish was to go there. The Kingdom of Swaziland, surrounded on three sides by South Africa and to the east by Mozambique. Spindly markings on the map stretched before her like nerves, and then southern Africa came to life. Vein-like rivers crossed a skeleton of boundaries, shading shaped the contours of mountains, a web of etchings and broken lines revealed roadways intersecting towns.

Cameron said authoritatively, "Swaziland has the last absolute monarchy in Africa." He sat erect, head poised forward as he questioned her knowledge of the region, her reasons for wanting to go.

She expressed sympathy for the poor, justice for the persecuted, the necessity for a socio-economic approach when implementing change.

"You have experience of working overseas?"

Six months' voluntary work at the U.K Aid charity shop hadn't exactly qualified her for the position of Programme Development Officer, and she had failed to mention she was half-Swazi in her covering letter. She should have managed things differently. But she was hooked by the quest to find family. He lolled back – a fisherman reeling in a catch. He cupped a large hand to his lips, subtly cleared his throat. Why travel so far? Give up the life she knows?

She talked impulsively of the southern African people's oppression, the need for democracy. "Half the Swazi nation follows the traditional way of life," she explained, "the other half is working to eliminate King Mswati."

"You've heard of Swaziland's freedom-fighter?"

"Sipho Matsebula."

"Sipho's a notorious troublemaker," Cameron snapped. Then he slipped with ease to the next subject and the mood in the room mellowed to induction mode. "U.K Aid, as you'll know, puts women and children first. Our mission as an NGO is to protect human rights. Our main focus areas are gender empowerment. Education. Health." He talked about the Development Officer's day-to-day tasks – monitoring projects, evaluating impact, the importance of research, writing thorough reports, the agency's hands-on approach, how most training took place in the field. His voice trailed away under the urgent ring of his telephone. He grasped the receiver. "Hello, Sindy? Yes."

His office overlooked the north edge of Lambeth Park. A Ferris wheel glittered in the late afternoon light, dominating the scene. Trees screened the rest of the fair with their leafy mosaic of ambers, pimentos, greenish-browns. Soon the clocks would go back and the days grow even shorter.

Cameron replaced the receiver and their eyes locked for a second. "Why do you want the job?" he asked.

"I want to help African people." That sounded crass.

The aromas of tobacco, wood polish and eau-de-Cologne spiced the office air.

His voice became tuned harmoniously with her emotions. "You're one of those people who believes Africa – an entire continent – is helpless without the West's support?"

"I didn't say that. Development can go wrong..." Rumpled and disarranged, she stuttered, "A-a-aid should be given without strings attached."

"Do you have any questions?" he said hurriedly.

She remained cowed. "Um, no." Tension and regret built. She should have done more research, come up with hard facts.

His eyes narrowed. "Why Swaziland in particular?"

"My father died... He was from there. I've always wanted to go – sorry." Her throat contracted. Why say that? Out of her depth she gulped, and swallowed only air. Applying for this job would have been out of the question when her father was alive. By mentioning him, she had removed emotional clothes. The damage was done. She would never hear back.

"Some applicants' qualifications are purely academic," a note of sympathy lifted Cameron's tone.

Koliwe tried to look calm, although, like a fragile ornament, she felt she would shatter if dropped. "I fear I'll become like Dad, detached, always living here in England."

"How long is it since you lost your dad?"

"Two months." Twisting her hands in the ends of her scarf, she focused upon her lap. "Of course, I only realised his importance..."

"...after he was gone," Cameron interrupted warmly. "That's often the way. You'll need to be gentle with yourself. Sometimes you'll wonder who you are, where you belong." His eyes went deep into hers, softly this time. "You really want this job, don't you?"

This man got what she was reaching for – a journey that would turn her inside out. "People think I can't put up with hardships, because I'm well-spoken and went to boarding school." She concentrated on the map, longing to dissolve into the mountains, to travel to the time and place of her father's parents. But the past was too solid. She was trembling at the edges. To steady herself she focused on the posters of malnourished children, their distended stomachs, protruding ribs, bloated heads, pleading eyes. "All I think about is *them*. Is their suffering our fault?"

Cameron's expression did not give a clue. He smiled charitably. Then looked up and away, as if the answers were written in pink mackerel clouds across the sky.

Her thigh muscles tensed. Emotions were shocks coursing her body. Although she grew up on English soil, a Swazi life she hadn't experienced ran through her veins. She clung to the chair. Alone in her home country. Alone in the world. She had tracked down Rachel – the aunt her father rarely mentioned. The aunt she had a right to know – from contact details held by the lawyer handling Moses' will. There was no telephone number, only a Johannesburg PO box address.

Shifting in the chair, she prepared to stand. "When will I hear?"

"About the job? Tomorrow." Cameron reached out a hand to shake. "That colour you're wearing suits you." Their hands clasped together. "Sindy," he called to the receptionist, "show Miss Dlamini out." He looked Koliwe in the eye as if they shared a secret. "See you very soon," he said with finality.

A flurry of news sheets bearing Princess Diana's worn face somersaulted over the pavement's large square slabs. *Death of a Princess* fluttered against the railings at the bottom of the stone steps. Crossing the road, Koliwe threaded between cars slow-moving as cattle, and the scent of deep-fried doughnuts and hot dogs with onions floated in the air.

*

"Dinner is served," calls Mrs Johnston from the dining room.

"Well announced!" cries the colonel.

The light fades fast, her sobriety with it. Outside, points of light sparkle from the darkness of mountains. The room reflected back is dense with guests and smoke. Cameron's greyish curls are higher than other guests' heads. From this hilltop, Mbabane is a jewel box. She feels tawdry close up, and as elusive as air. Yet she experiences a sudden sense of elation. Swaziland, at last.

The dinner table is a bleary haze of rich food and expensive wines. Mrs. Johnston has arranged silver candelabras across the white linen tablecloth. Candles lit, Clotilda's eyes sparkle. A diamond necklace and earrings spray her alabaster skin with glittering crystalline drops.

Jeanette's breasts threaten to burst from her dress as she picks up her wine glass. "We often have big family dos with my sisters and their children," Jeanette says, nudging Clotilda. "We have a nice bungalow in one of the former white suburbs with a garden and an open bar."

"Often we have family parties of fifty or more, with my sisters, brothers, their wives and children," Clotilda cuts in, with a mincing tone. "On Monday, I was so full from the last night's braai, I couldn't take breakfast. After our dogs had sniffed at the boerewors and bacon, I had to throw them out to Mimi, the maid."

Howls of laughter make naked candle flames billow and shudder. Mrs Johnston seats herself beside Koliwe. Everything Mrs Johnston says seems to be double-edged. Koliwe tries to ask where it is safe to go, whether she should drive alone, but her hostess is absorbed in conversation with Martin, and Cameron has migrated to the far end of the table. Koliwe turns to Clotilda, who basks in glimmering candlelight on her other side.

"For what we are about to receive," Mrs Johnston gracefully bows her head, "may the Lord make us truly grateful."

Amens ripple around the dining room.

Unfolding his napkin, the colonel makes a broad gesture with his hand across the tabletop, indicating the food. "Do start everybody. Bon appétit."

Heads bow with intent and there are satisfied munching sounds. Koliwe notices with muted horror the other guests' slanting looks. She tries a polite smile. A maid brings four wine bottles from a cooler and sloshes wine into glasses.

"Swaziland's problem is AIDS," John says to Koliwe. "One man has three, maybe four girlfriends and each of his girlfriends has three or four boyfriends. If that first man is HIV positive, he passes the virus to all his girlfriends, who pass it on to their boyfriends. That's how HIV spreads. A tap's been left on, U.K Aid's programmes can only mop up the mess."

"How insensitive can you be, John darling," Clotilda says, "when we've just had the worst flood in our house? All your talk of mopping up messes..." She leans towards Koliwe conspiratorially. "Last year, when the rains came, acres of our gardens were utterly destroyed. Roses, all in flower, ruined. Worst day ever."

"Haven't your roses grown back?" Koliwe asks.

"Books can be claimed through insurance. Furnishings can be dried. *You can't dry roses!*"

"I have experience of many countries and cultures of Africa," Martin proffers – he must be on his second bottle of red. "On my travels, I've developed a keen interest in African fiction and poetry, making it my vocation to learn about, read and meet as many African writers as I can."

The colonel looks over his shoulder anxiously, snorting, "Where's the maid?" She is nowhere to be seen. He grabs an antique silver platter from the warmer to replenish guests' plates with vegetables, bestowing carrots and green beans generously, finishing the round with his wife. As if she has a long-standing fear of being poisoned, she avoids the food he serves by positioning it neatly in a pile at the plate's edge.

"You've heard what Sipho Matsebula said about the love test?" Clotilda directs her question at Martin.

When Koliwe repeats, "Sipho Matsebula?" all heads turn to her.

"He isn't helping anyone except himself," Martin adds, with beaming face. "Let them have their king, his wives, the unfairness, his hypocrisy. Let them have their mud huts and spears. All the kaffirs want is a bloodbath." His face glows ruddy; his red-rimmed eyes fill with malice, and he chuckles uneasily. "Hei, only joking of course."

Clotilda applauds, her jewellery twinkling in the shrunken candles' light.

The colonel blurts out, "Tribalism's all wrong."

"African leaders are corrupt and inept," his wife cuts across.

"Hei, first things first," Martin exclaims, "and the first step is for the king to remove that ring from his nose!"

Discomfort drips through Koliwe's veins. More wine flows. The Swaziland she glimpsed in her father's stories – children with polished mealie-fattened faces, their hair plaited painfully neat – simply isn't here. To have thought she would be at home in his birth place was a naïve dream.

Dessert is another guilt trip – a marshmallowy tart coated in dark chocolate with a sweet Moscato d'Asti to drink.

Guests migrate from the dining room to a stately drawing room, fanning out across a silk Kashmir rug. A maid glides around with a cheeseboard bearing a soft and hard selection, crackers and fruits. Cameron emerges from a cluster sipping liqueur at the opposite end of the room.

Koliwe has been chatting drunkenly to a woman in a silky, strapless, navy-blue dress that flows to the floor like a waterfall. Did the woman say her name was Maureen? Glossy

31

locks frame her pretty shoulders; marble eyes set in a porcelain face. Maureen's accent is intriguing. Koliwe cannot distinguish where it is from; snatches break into odd words, hint, and waver through sentences intermittently. The drawing room swirls; Koliwe's balance is off.

Cameron's eyes hover over her face and away, with the blue-green flash of a dragonfly. He is an oasis of calm. With the trace of a smile, he cocks his head closer to hers, and says intuitively, "These people can drag one down."

Silently, she nods, and combs knotted strands of hair that want taming. Heading for the doorway, she catches Colonel Johnston's sleeve. "Thank you for a lovely evening."

The colonel grins, strutting like a cockerel across the verandah.

"Yes, it was," his wife repeats, "lovely."

The turquoise-blue swimming pool is illuminated by underwater lights. The Johnstons call the guard to escort Koliwe to a taxi, but the guard has gone to feed the dogs. Koliwe goes out alone.

The majestic wall of mountains stands stoic in the pearly darkness of moonlight. Lightning still crackles above the ridges; instead of breaking, the storm is moving further away. There is an extraordinary beauty to this vast landscape, even at night. Her father had talked of the land as *inkomo*, the beast of the nation, and the hills take on the shapes of animals as though they are alive – to her they certainly seem to be, with their high-ridged backs and curved shapes stretching to eternity.

The distance to the taxi rank is barely decreasing. The ground is strangely alien beneath her feet; a spinning sensation replaces gravity – she is orbiting earth from space. She glances back to the house lit up by lanterns stuck in the neatly mown lawn. Something jolts within her. The expat life will not include her. No invitations to the Country Club will ever arrive. The realisation comes almost as a relief, and yet leaves her feeling fragile. The distant mass of mountainous rock is magnified, mocks her with its power and dignity. It has taken on a character she is reacting to and resisting against; even as she is drawn in, she finds herself wanting to fight back. The moon above, an eye, follows her every move.

Engine purring, a rusted red Land Rover rattles towards the gateway and draws up alongside her.

"Koliwe," Cameron calls, "want a lift?"

She has trouble judging where her feet should go as she clambers into the passenger seat.

"You're staying at Pine View Flats?"

"That's right," she replies drowsily.

Cameron's shadow looms across her; as Project Coordinator, he wields enormous power. Timidly, Koliwe smiles; now they are alone together.

The guard, shrinking from the intense glare of the Land Rover's beam, punches numbers into a pin pad to activate the electric gates. Koliwe glances over her shoulder and across Mbabane, hoping her dream of a new life in Swaziland will not appear like the city lights, which appear somehow changed. Menacing.

An Alsatians' eyes wink red in the guard's torchlight. The headlights pour two silvery streams through the darkness as the vehicle moves steadily onto the road.

"Most of the land here is owned by blacks," Cameron says, firmly gripping the steering wheel. He has put on a tan leather bomber jacket. "Land disputes are commonplace. You'll know all about that, of course."

"My dad never talked about these things." Ashamed of her ignorance, she swallows the knot tightening her throat.

Cameron seems to know everything about Swaziland; everything she wants to understand.

Her father had said he was from the Dlamini clan. A question drifts to the front of her mind. "What's the difference between a clan and a tribe?"

"A clan is a related group of people. A tribe shares the same cultural values, yet may not be related at all."

"My surname, Dlamini, I've noticed, is common here. Is the king always a Dlamini?"

"The king comes from the largest clan, Dlamini," Cameron continues to explain. "You'll see," he forewarns, "there's antagonism towards the monarchy."

Gazing at the dark city streets she wonders whether her family are related to the monarchy.

"And your name is Xolile Dlamini…" he says.

Hearing her name pronounced with the authentic Xhosa click, she experiences a weird sensation of drifting through the past. She navigates her tongue around different sounds – *Kohleeway Koliwe Xolile* – mouthing her own name. Then she is swamped by a real sense of failure. "Dad came from Swaziland. He was only eighteen when he left. I was born in England. To me, as a child, this country was barely more than a name."

She catches her reflection in the window, imposed upon the shapes of office blocks, shacks, trees. Her bushy hair blown about like a thicket of tumbleweed.

"Have you family here?" Cameron inquires.

"An aunt. Rachel. I'm trying to find her, though I don't have an address." She curls a strand of hair behind an ear, then sits on her fingers, pressing them tightly down.

All around is darkness now the moon is hidden by cloud.

"You went to boarding school." Cameron's gaze remains fixed on the road. His gold watch winks in the dashboard's glow as he rotates his wrist. "Expensive. Very."

They cruise through a side street of closed kiosks and old wooden houses on stilts.

She opens the window wider. Warm air blasts across her forehead and messes with her hair. When she looks up, the mountain walls are vaguely visible, jagged against a moonless sky, then the topmost ridges give way to darkness. The loneliness stirring within her mixes with fear and want. She fears the shape of things to come. Fears strange beasts will skulk out from thickets. Fears the weight of the unknown, where the pitch black within her is blacker than the night.

After saying goodbye, she ascends the silent staircase, unlocks the bedsit door. Feeling flattened like a portrait or a photograph, she gazes at the street below. Boys, swanking along, dissolve into darkness. Her fingers touch her mother's precious necklace. If she could reach with her hand back through the past six years, clutch one of those sleepy summery days at the cottage near Oxford with her mother and transport her encapsulated in that time to here, Koliwe would do so, for the lights which guide her are dim.

The faint hope of finding her aunt, Rachel, glimmers.

Then she is running through the silver-grey mist of rain. Is she saving her father's life? Or causing him to fall?

CHAPTER TWO

The bedsit consists of two poorly furnished rooms. From the dingy kitchenette, with its sickly, cloying urine smell, a door leads to a small pantry and an archway opens onto the combined bedroom and sitting room. Two windows secured by burglar bars let in the floating jacaranda fragrance. The front window overlooks Allister Miller Street, Mbabane's main thoroughfare, where ragged groups of Swazi men drink and argue outside a row of restaurants, shops, public houses. Morning sunshine throws light upon the clear view from the back across the mountains' rugged ravines and valleys.

The bed Koliwe lies in is pushed against the wall. A light bulb coated in dust dangles from the centre of the ceiling. Twisting her neck on the pillow, she looks up. Cracks climb the walls to the ceiling, interlinking like roads, and memories emerge like lines on a map. Above her head, the paintwork is blotched, with furls the pasty colour of the parchment paper her father used; it always curled at the edges before he pinned it to a frame.

She flares with anger, thinking once again of *him*. She had wanted to see his birthplace, to touch what was their past. And she thinks of him colouring in the years of her life. At times, he had lived for his brushes and paints. Quiet and constant as the river each summer, painting the present, obscuring the past. He *should* have brought her. There is a sense of fulfilment, lying in bed, as though divided halves of herself are finally merging.

The toilet and shower are off the landing. Sharing a bathroom is an indignity – she cannot say this to anyone openly, having chosen to live in this basic accommodation, amongst the poorer local community. Cockroaches scuttle into corners when she clambers from the bed, a dank odour rises from where the linoleum has cracked, but the floor, already heated by the sun, is warm beneath the soles of her feet.

In the bathroom mirror, she faces the woman she longs to be. There, at Heathrow, was the ghost of a girl, surrounded by absent goodbyes, a fear of never finding family clouding her mind. Despite attempts to 'pass', school teachers regarded her as exotic. Other. Shunted, unwanted, from one friendship to another. As an adolescent, she dreamed she could slip from her skin to watch herself from outside. That strange phenomenon has haunted her ever since arriving.

Today is Saturday. Monday will be her first day at work. She cleans the bedsit thoroughly, tying scarves in her colours of jade and magenta to conceal chafed varnish on the battered furniture. She polishes the flimsy ply-board dressing table; the drawers stick and have to be shunted open. The bottom drawer, where her paints are stored, reeks of mouldering rubber. Her six Russian dolls are arranged across the chest of drawers. Sunlight trickles between the window bars as she sets up the easel.

But she first decides to go out to stock up with shopping and breakfast, and leaves the sheet of plain white paper ready for her return. Locking the door, she ventures along the landing, downstairs and into the fast-food joint across the road.

Apart from the staff, the place is deserted. The menu is chalked on a blackboard behind the service desk: Pap, meat pies, gravy, boerewors, droëwors, Russians and chips, walkie talkies (chicken feet), vetkoek and mince.

"What's that?" she asks at the hot food counter.

"Bunny-chow," the woman replies. The dish in the stainless-steel platter is a kind of stew stuffed into a loaf of bread. The woman points to a pie, then something resembling mashed potato, and says, "Vetkoek. Chicken wings. Pap."

Shamed, Koliwe recoils. Hunger shrinks. She hands over twenty rand – an unwelcome guest picked out by the sharp brightness of fluorescent strips.

On the street, a woman pushes briskly past, a baby clinging to her chest. Like a little chimp, Koliwe thinks, and slams into a boy crawling on his knees, hands clasped up to passers-by in prayer. Hastily, she swerves from him. Something frightful is about to descend. In England, AIDS DON'T DIE OF IGNORANCE, are distributed to all households. Here, AIDS attacks not only gay men and drug addicts, it attacks everyone. The fear is wrong. HIV, she knows, is not airborne, but it is still unnerving to roam streets where so many carry a fatal virus.

"Hey! Hey!" yells a man, brilliant, red wing feathers stick out proudly from his traditional warrior headdress, fluttering when he moves. "Hey, my costume, take photograph."

She peers at him over the rims of her sunglasses.

"I give you souvenir for your stay." The man holds out something shiny.

She is curious and somewhat amused. "What is it?"

"Beautiful ring."

"How much? The price. How much?"

The sun winks from behind the man's head. "For you, is free. I give you ring." He strokes the triangle of hair beneath his lower lip. "Ring I give to marry."

She thanks him, says, "*No*," firmly.

"Is lonely, I know. My wife dead." He twiddles his moustache ends, strokes his goatee again and tries a different tack. "Hey, why you half-black African and half-white, girl?" The man tilts his head. "I love you. You beautiful." He catches her arm. "You. Me. Have good fuck."

Sweating face mottled red, she braces indignantly. Walks away purposefully. Glances over her shoulder. The man is weaving in the opposite direction through scurrying shoppers; the strings of seeds wound around his ankles rattle. The bustling street has become a desert. Intimacy and loneliness grow, spiky cactus flowers seek solace in the shady concrete warren of crimson bungalows, pastel-coloured split-level houses, shabby office blocks and rickety tin shacks with corrugated iron roofs. She steps nimbly around a girl in a ragged, charcoal-streaked dress, wedged between a mattress and a mud-patched wall, sneaking food from a bowl into her mouth. The girl's eyes no longer hold the glimmer of hope.

The sun's heat intensifies. Blinking through beads of sweat, Koliwe sets off for the supermarket in the wrong direction, turning left into a side street instead of right. Someone moves into her peripheral vision. The warrior man again? Unaccustomed to so many hawkers, she steps onto the pavement from the road. No one knows her name or face. At every corner she expects to bump into her father. Trying not to think about him has the opposite effect. Is that him in the hectic marketplace, or crossing too close to a car? Are any of these people related to her?

She purchases what she wants. Dumps shopping on the bedsit breakfast bar.

U.K Aid's headquarters occupy a high-rise concrete building on the same street as the British High Commission. Union Jacks hang limply against the blue, windless Monday morning sky. Two security men in khaki uniforms, similarly listless, guard either side of the door. The reception area is vast, the walls smoky grey.

"That way to the lift." The receptionist sticks out her arm like a signpost.

Koliwe is captivated by the woman's hairstyle; it looks as though a black towel has been coiled around her head and balances, tight and conical.

The lift doors slide apart, revealing buttons for the five floors. Time has a telescoping effect. Her father's eyes stare from her face as the cubicle glides up. Her frostiness for him does not fade – like lightning striking mother and father – through summer's sulphur shades or violent violet winters.

Telephones ring, demanding to be answered, as the lift doors pull apart. The granite floor is as glassy as polished marble. Solid black lettering and a logo on a gleaming brass plaque indicate the main U.K Aid office.

A lean woman in her late thirties rises from a desk. "Sawubona," she says.

Koliwe recognises the greeting but cannot recall how to reply.

"I'm Phepile, Project Coordinator. How was your journey?" Phepile carries a quiet dignity. Laughter lines are etched around her deep-set eyes; her hair is a tight bonnet of curls.

The offices, quiet, green-carpeted spaces, are smaller than Koliwe had expected. Sunshine blazes through the windows, illuminating wall maps of Swaziland. Medical projects are the main thrust of U.K Aid's work; the network of lines and pinpointed locations show the branch has a wide reach.

"We're so happy you're here, you'll reduce our workload." Phepile clutches a clipboard to her breast. "Come, Xolile." She uses the Xhosa click. "I'll show you what I mean."

Koliwe replies, "Oh, call me Koliwe, please," mispronouncing her own name.

The intensity of Philipe's stare stings Koliwe for her arrogance.

Koliwe. Xolile. Whose name is it anyway?

Phepile says, "I'll introduce the rest of the team," showing her through to a back-office.

Koliwe's high cheek-boned face, anxiously angled to one side, resembles an obedient puppy. Navigating her way between the computers dotted about the room, she follows Phepile's spritely walk. Three women, their relationships forged by shared experience, greet her in chorus – "Sawubona" – and shake her hand.

"Hlengiwe, Gender Empowerment Officer." Hlengiwe is wide-eyed, with leathery patches of skin on her cheeks.

"Katerina, I work in Health." Katerina's fleshy face has slits for eyes that gleam like polished obsidian. She gives an 'OK' thumb-to-index finger sign.

The third, Sambulo, has silvered ebony hair plaited in cornrows. Her skin smiles with the fluid sheen of black oil. "Education's my area." Sambulo runs her fingers along the lines where her brown scalp shows.

To look at Phepile is like facing a bright sun. Pushing out her triangular chin, she beams at Koliwe, owning the space. "Our projects are divided into three categories: in the pipeline; ongoing; winding up." Lists on a board endorse Phepile's words. "The categories are subdivided into groups." Phepile thrusts a sheaf of papers at Koliwe. "These outline the main issues we're working on. Food security. The general poverty project. The effects of HIV and AIDS on health, education and OVCs."

Koliwe's forehead wrinkles. "OVCs?"

"Orphans and Vulnerable Children." Phepile tosses the clipboard on the mess of manila folders on a Formica table top.

Determined to make a difference, Koliwe catches herself smiling at the prospect of future responsibilities.

"We're short-staffed." Phepile's voice becomes hushed. "My husband, Teri, he's too sick to work. Allen, my brother-in-law, was our driver. Lost him six months ago." Her face narrows, lips tighten, eyebrows pinch together. "Only last week we buried Allen's second wife. Three of my sisters passed away within weeks of each other, leaving behind many children." A muscle plays in Phepile's cheek, her mouth pulls down at the corners, darkening her face. "Swaziland's HIV rate is the highest in the world and the numbers testing positive only rise."

Koliwe stops grinning. She has studied the statistics. This is the reality.

Phepile saunters past Koliwe with a fevered expression and desolate eyes. "*Never* has a country recorded such large numbers of parentless kids," she throws over her shoulder.

41

"What will become of them?"

"Who can say?" Phepile hands over a UN report. "Life expectancy has almost halved in ten years."

Koliwe feels as flimsy as the pages of figures she is flicking through. The CEOs, directors, trustees in U.K Aid's brochures are white men like Cameron. The local black female staff perform fieldwork, research, secretarial tasks. Aware of her skin colour, flushed and freckled as her mother's, the burden of linking lives, hopes and expectations with financial contributions rest heavily.

Phepile's tone radiates with integrity. "You'll learn about HIV' s effects. Check the clinic nurses' test results are sent for analysis. Keep records up to date."

Koliwe nips in enthusiastically, "What about better sanitation, improved water supplies to villages?"

Phepile, turning her back, busies herself with another task. "We'll get you out interviewing child-headed families, then you'll engage with communities at grassroots level." She throws over her shoulder, "Mr Callow might give you a different brief when he returns. Until then, anything you need, any problems, come to me."

"Mr Callow isn't here?" Koliwe manages to slip in.

"No." Phepile directs her to a desk wedged between a wall and a filing cabinet. "That cabinet," Phepile says firmly, "is mine, remember."

"But Mr Callow's the branch head."

"Sadly, he had to fly to London. You've missed him by only a couple of days." Phepile yanks open the top drawer of the filing cabinet, selects two folders. "You'll regularly meet with other key people. Contacts are in here." She waggles the folders in the air then slips them back into the cabinet.

CHAPTER THREE

Koliwe slithers into an olive-green dress, bundles curl up from the nape of her neck and, tossing her head forwards, ties a magenta and midnight blue scarf into a stylish wrap.

By the end of the first week, she has read the year's project reports and been allocated a word processor. She wants to accomplish as much as she can as Programme Development Officer, but she struggles with the computer; it whirs like the one her father used.

She slides her gold-rimmed glasses from their case. Memories dwell in every corner. Then she is back in his lofty studio with a high roof with two skylights. She is eight years old. That winter the heating worked, so it was warm in the daytime, but cold when they stayed in the evenings. After her father switched off the boiler, they huddled over the fan heater. He told her complementary colours never clash. Colour circles pinned on the walls showed a rainbow of shades. He was working on the watercolours stored in folders in drawers. He daubed a frosted landscape methodically. The pure stench of turpentine clung to her clothes. She dawdled by racks of paintings of haylofts, haystacks, apple blossom, the blighted blossom on the cherry; sable brushes hoarded in jugs in the cherrywood chest. Sketch pads strewn across the floor. She could flick through the years of his life – sometimes drawn, sometimes written.

Later, he worked in the cottage. The study had a warm and wonderful smell, linseed oil and varnish mingled with a musty odour of whisky. There were tubes in boxes on stacks of newspapers. Square-ended brushes stiffened with paint, jutted from jars and buckled tins with torn labels advertising peach slices, pear halves. Moses could not find paid work. In London, police stopped and searched him in the street. But, as his collections of paintings grew, he put on exhibitions. He had an exhibition of York and its surroundings. Views of the North Yorkshire Moors in various lights. The shifting moods of the River Ouse – the lissom willow, prolific along the banks, trailing leafy limbs into the water – to intriguing, narrow alleyways; the sudden magnificent medieval building from the city's illustrious past.

She strolls through an area of single-storey ranch houses. Still hears the grandfather clock in the hall – tick-tock, tick-tock – brown, like her father, familiar, tall. His voice is as close as her thoughts, as close as her breath. His spirit moves with her. Is this country home? A beggar reaches out across the pavement; a leper waves an arm stump. Barefoot children offer to shine her shoes. Her mind quietly holds the image of a child she passed, crouched low on his hands and knees amidst the litter, lapping oily brackish water from an overflowing gutter. All at once her worries seem trivial.

Back at British Aid's offices, Phepile hands Koliwe a cardboard box. "*Cooldrink*, sandwiches, biscuits."

"For me?" Koliwe asks.

Phepile laughs quietly. "You must eat, Xolile."

Clutching their lunches, Phepile and Koliwe glide in the lift to the ground floor, down concrete stairs and across the car park. Koliwe fast walks to escape the heat, but Phepile, with her dignified grace, moves faster.

Phepile breathes a smoky sigh from her nostrils, inches the car into the stream of traffic and little by little, they move through Mbabane's suburbs, an intricate wilderness.

"This isn't far from where I worked as a kid," Phepile says. The road narrows to one lane and winds up hilly, leafy avenues. The air is cooler. Villas and mansions replace the shacks and tenement blocks on the urban periphery. "I detest the rich part of town," she says. "Millionaire's retreat. Diplomats and politicians stop here. There's security cameras, golden gates. It looks nice to newcomers but" – she sucks on a cigarette with the seriousness of a child sucking milk through a straw – "you only find black housekeepers working for white Africans here."

The car chugs up the slope, tops the highest hill on the outskirts of Mbabane and flat landscape replaces the confines of office blocks. Treeless fields slip by, the soil eroded by toxic fertilisers – shortcuts to grow cash crops. On the horizon, the tall chimneys of industry belch ashen fumes into the sun-bleached sky. Women cook maize by the roadside. Girls hold out handmade earrings: polished jade, ivory and ebony beads dangle in bunches from their fingers like dates from palm trees. On either side of the road are glimpses of other lives. Of alternatives. Of the immeasurable freedom of passing miles.

Small groups of men and women stand by the roadside. Women dressed in orange and red, the brightly patterned cloth knotted on one shoulder. One man raises his knobkerrie in a kind of salutation and yells "Hei!" at Phepile. Phepile smiles in return. Boys herd stray goats, browsing in the sunlight glancing on the valleys.

The car bounces across a rutted wooden bridge, the dirt road ends and Phepile pulls up. On foot, they thread through a ramshackle settlement poised on a steep slope. It will take over an hour to reach their destination. Phepile is quiet, her presence comforting. They rest by an abandoned rondavel in the umbra of a flame tree planted long ago for shade.

Grasslands, dotted with shrubs, spread east to west; a river gleams jealous green. White smoke coils from smallholdings scattered in a valley's undulating folds. Further down the track, children are holed up in a makeshift hovel like rabbits in a hutch. They look broken, hunkered behind the sharp teeth of a tin shack.

"How do those children survive?" Koliwe asks.

Phepile's deep-set eyes squint. "You mean, where do they find food and shelter when their parents have died," comes her rhetorical answer.

Koliwe does not reply. Like Phepile, sitting on the grass eating sandwiches, she relies on a salary. Together, they are dependent on aid.

Shaking her head, "Ehe," Phepile utters, as she reads case notes, eyebrows arched high with concern.

She tells Koliwe about the girl they are visiting. "Thandiwe's the eldest child, she had to nurse her dying mother and sister, and care for three siblings. Her first husband died. I'd say her second husband's a bully."

"Is Thandiwe attending school?" There is a faint fizz as Koliwe brings the Coca-Cola can to her lips. When she takes a swig, she feels bright sunlight through closed eyelids.

"School fees are high," Phepile says. "Thandiwe eats cabbage and mealie-meal porridge. Cabbage one day, porridge the next, then cabbage then porridge for many weeks. Thandiwe had to choose — education or food. Girls like Thandiwe sell their clothes, pots, pans, firewood, goats. Everything. They even sell themselves, become whores for just ten rand."

Koliwe digs the toe of her sandal into the gravel, making small movements of grit and stones.

"I'm Thandiwe's lihlombe lekukhalela," Phepile announces.

Koliwe wipes sweat from her questioning face.

"A shoulder to cry on," Phepile translates.

The track narrows to a grassy path. Koliwe's legs work mechanically.

Phepile is at home; her pinched face as weathered as the ancient rocks as the surrounding mountains. "Heyi, for Thandiwe, each day is a difficult one. Having a friend to talk to helps. Life's hard. If you're living positive, HIV will kill you." Phepile's low voice is husky and dry, "Men are free to do anything. There's no law to stop them. Some men believe virginity's a cure, that virgins cleanse them."

Dust blows into their eyes and hair as they descend to a shanty village. A sign outside a church says: God is Good. An aged woman with a peevish frown sits in the doorway to a roadside bar, a little girl pinned between her knees. The woman's skin is crumpled cloth; she has empty, sagging bags for breasts. She yanks the child's hair into stiff plaits.

Phepile points to an iron shack cradled in the curve of a river. The distant *dhu, dhu, dhu* of a pestle and mortar floats on the air.

Banana trees throw shadows across the yard they approach. A girl in a lilac dress patterned with lime-green flowers shelters beneath the leaves. Standing, the girl steps forwards; stern eyes and sharp face thought-absorbed, like the stout-billed marabou stork picking through the swamp.

Koliwe is taking in Thandiwe's unusually light brown eyes; the irises glint amber like gemstones.

"Thandi," Phepile says tenderly to the girl, "I've brought a visitor to see you, Xolile."

"Yes," says Thandi mindfully. She glances across Koliwe's loose blouse, jeans, open-toed sandals. She apologises, "My English is no good."

Flies orbit Thandi's plaited and beaded shoulder-length hair; her arms glitter with opaque sand specks. She dusts down her knees, then her bare feet patter across the yard to the shack. Two boys hover in the doorway, clutching toy cars fashioned from scrap metal, and a tiny schoolgirl in a turquoise tunic hops and skips from her own shadow. Thandi speaks to the children. They scramble onto a plank held up by oil drums and sit and watch Koliwe.

The air inside the shack is stale, funky and hot. The room – there is only one – contains two folding metal chairs; a steel table peeling yellow paint; a bed; a pitifully thin pillow. Thandi untangles blankets; shakes dead flies crawling with maggots from the middle a brown-looking sheet.

Phepile says discreetly to Thandi, "Are you okay?"

Thandi wipes her mud-streaked forehead with the back of her hand. Koliwe's attention flits from Phepile back to Thandi. Sunlight captures the glass and copper beads, glistening like raindrops, threaded through Thandi's hair.

"When did you last eat?" Phepile asks.

Tears well in Thandi's eyes. "My chickens have been stolen. Cows ate my crops, leaving nothing to harvest." After straightening the bedding, she moves on spindly legs, one hand clearing up drifts of dirty clothes, the other shielding a bruised cheek. Her expression says she has fallen over the edge of hunger. Heat and worry have sapped her strength. Want has eaten her pride. Her shame goes deep, but the fear in her eyes goes deeper.

"Yes, I need food," Thandi replies, drying her eyes.

Phepile hands the girl the third lunch box.

Sunlight blurs into shadow in the corner where Thandi cowers; her forearms are as scaly as the salt fish sold in Mbabane marketplace. Clutching her stomach, chewing silently; her face, tense, she concentrates on the sandwiches, as though the food quells not only hunger but also misery and pain.

Phepile's feet are planted solidly on the mud floor. "Thandi," she continues, "tell Koliwe about your family. Koliwe, come, sit."

Thandi shrinks further into the corner. Dark and still, Koliwe perches beside Phepile, taking in the dismal atmosphere, the ravenous girl.

"I need help. With everything." Thandi counts each item on her fingertips: "Washing, mending, sweeping, gathering firewood, watering goats, baking scones to sell at the school gates, making peace between my brothers when they fight like rats over scraps." Thandi swigs from a goatskin flask. "I'll tell you about my mother's illness." Eyes flashing to Koliwe, devouring sandwiches as she talks: "The sangoma said she would cure Mama by giving her muti to snort, and a herbal remedy to wash in. She said I must bring herbs for her medicines in exchange for the muti and spells. The white nurse, who smells of chemicals like the local clinic, hadn't visited for months. She brought food, and told me: 'Burn everything the sangoma gave you, Jesus has come into your life, the demons will vanish.'"

Koliwe shuffles across the bed to be closer to the girl.

Hiding tears, Thandi bows her head. Her lips twist with worry. "I heard Papa shouting before I saw him coming over the hill. I was herding the goats in. The pills Mama took needed food. But we had nothing to eat. I knew the fever had taken over when I found Mama lying perfectly still, like a doll, there, on our sleeping mat. The bag of bones beside the pot was Thula, my sister." Thandi swipes flies feasting at the corners of her eyes. "I couldn't watch Mama and Thula die. But I couldn't leave them." She asks Koliwe, "You think they lived?"

Koliwe nods gravely.

"You lie to yourself," whispers Thandi. "Papa couldn't pay for funerals. He packed his bag and left." Thandi blinks tears back. "Without Papa, I couldn't feed myself, Precious, my other sister, and my brothers."

Phepile's cheeks swell like dumplings. She says firmly, comfortingly, "Weeping won't bring your parents back. I'm here for you, Thandi, my dear."

Thandi's face is grey. Stiffly, she stands, then sits beside Koliwe on the bed. From the mattress she takes up a red shawl, clutches it to her chest, hangs her head; her body shakes pitifully. Patterns from palm tree fronds, projected inside the shack, play impetuously, shuddering in the breeze, like the fingers of a scrawny child scratching at the walls. Caged in misery.

Phepile stabs Koliwe with her finger. Koliwe rips her gaze away and prickles with guilt for staring at Thandi.

Thandi turns to Koliwe. "HIV's a demon. You never know when the killer demon will strike. This demon you cannot see. It lurks in thorn bushes. Takes your spirit. Stalks women at night. Some say, 'so and so caught this thing', but really this thing caught so and so. You fight the demon, you lose. Marriage won't protect you. If men wear a condom the demon attacks – many people believe this. Men say sex with a condom's like sucking a sweet with the wrapper on. You think umlungu – white people – are safe. You thought the demon couldn't cross the river. It did."

Phepile guides Thandi back to her story, "Tell Xolile about your first husband."

"I met him in town. He looked me up and down, said he'd seen me outside the homestead. He stared at the private part between my legs. Sometimes he waited by the school gates. He said he worked at the sugar plantation. Said he'd soon be rich. Said he'd take me to shop for clothes in South Africa. We'd drive there by car."

Phepile asks hurriedly, "You believed all that?"

Nodding, Thandi lowers her head. "This man told me Papa said I must marry. That night I left Precious, my sister, my twin brothers, Buzwe and Dumisa." She crosses her arms on her chest. "Everything was stinking in his shack. His bed was filthy. He slapped the smile from my face. He beat me as though I was a dog. I punched his head against the wall. Shoved him outside, slammed the door. Two days later he was back. All the food in my belly turned to water. Each day when I saw him, my belly was twisting. Most days I squatted in bushes. Most nights I collapsed. I couldn't eat or sleep. When he found out, *he* accused *me* of infecting *him!* But he was infected before we met. He isn't afraid of the wasting disease. He is afraid of gossip. These men are like pumpkins with vines spreading all over the ground, they spread themselves widely between many girls. Most girls are cabbages sitting alone, waiting for a man to come and pick them. My husband picked many girlfriends."

"Aren't you too young to be married?" Koliwe asks tentatively.

Thandi looks down. In the red shawl, she cradles an imaginary baby.

"What happened to your baby?" asks Phepile.

"Landa? My husband hid her behind grain sacks stacked at the back of his shack. I cried so much he hit me. He swore he'd find a rope to hang me if I ran away." Thandi twists the shawl into a rope.

Koliwe sees Thandi longs for the soft quiver of her baby snoring in her arms.

"One morning I woke to find my husband lying perfectly still. Like Thula. Like Mama. Like Landa." Thandi's voice trembles. "My mother-in-law said I must remarry." Thandi looks terrified, as though she is being stalked by a shapeless beast. "I'm going to have another baby." Sobbing, Thandi collapses on the mattress. "My new husband threatens to sell me to other men."

Phepile speaks to Thandi with such deep attentive affection, that tears glisten in her own eyes. "I hope the weight will lift from your heart."

Thandi is submerged in loss, each breath strangled. Gently, Koliwe rubs Thandi's back.

Phepile stands, hands on hips, watching Thandi's darting eyes, hunched shoulders. Phepile's expression says she is used to seeing girls at the mercy of predatory men. "You'll cope without family. You gain strength from friends like Nofoto, who've ploughed and planted in your newly-fenced garden."

There is a resemblance between Phepile and Thandi. The girl's filth and tear-streaked cheeks are softer than Phepile's; her eyes, lighter, but a steadfast determination defines their mutual defiance.

One of the boys has crept indoors, his nostrils flare beneath his peaked cap. He squats on his heels in a corner, watching his

51

older sister with inquisitive eyes.

Phepile says to Thandi, "I'll tell our nurses to bring food parcels."

The boy tugs Thandi's sleeve. She gets to her feet, waves away the haze of mosquitoes gossiping around her brother's head. He withdraws his precious toy car from the bib pocket of his grease-smeared overalls.

Waiting for Phepile to signal when to leave, Koliwe dusts the film of dirt from her jeans. Phepile folds Thandi's waif-like form into her arms then gives a sad smile of departure .

The warmth of Koliwe's hug spreads. Connecting through grief, Thandi's shoulders relax. She smells of warm milk; soft tufts of her hair brush Koliwe's cheek.

Sunlight blazes behind Precious. Holding the pleated skirt of her tunic over her knees, she squats. It is safe to retrieve her doll, hidden beneath the bed. She places the doll on a sleeping mat, touches the plastic arm, watches the body for a sigh, willing breath to come. Thandi lifts her sister with the doll into her arms as if they weigh nothing. Following Phepile and Koliwe into hot, dry sunshine, Thandi sets Precious down beneath the shady banana trees.

Phepile and Koliwe's backs turn on Thandi, a sunken shape in the doorway – her face a wooden mask carved by anguish; moon-shaped eyes white with fear; shoulders shrunk into her chest, rubbing her hands together, staring past them and into searing blue heat. Days are splintered. Her future up here in the hills flickers. Koliwe's conviction of saving lives and assuaging others' pain diminishes with each step. This acquisition of knowledge is the pouring of light into her mind.

"This is a place of memories," Phepile says, once they are out of earshot. "Memories and hunger. Many have been driven to leave. Those remaining are tied to grief and the gathering darkness."

"What will Thandi do? Her Mama's dead. Her Papa's in

South Africa. Her brothers? The white nurse?"

"Her gogo, aunts and uncles fear the demon will attack them. Her best friend, Nofoto, and Nofoto's youngest son, will die when the beast strikes them."

Hands thrust deep in her pockets, heading towards the car, a blue fleck on a distant hillside, Koliwe glances back along the thin grassy path to Thandi's shack. The wind burrows through grasses, making them shiver, as though something terrible is tunnelling towards the girl. Could this be the tokoloshe? A clever and evil spirit come to cause mischief and more trouble in Thandi's world?

"You know why these girls have so many babies?" Phepile asks in her steady voice. "When men are bored and they live in the city, they switch on the TV. When men are bored in the countryside, they make these girls open their legs." She inhales on a cigarette, gets into the car. "Women are born under suspicion," she says. "To be a woman here is to be a witch. People might say: Your sister-in-law is a witch – she has no children. A man can't love a wife who fails to bear him even one child. Women bring great shame. Shame to the household. Shame to the homestead. Shame to the family." She flicks the cigarette butt into grasses.

Memories Koliwe had wanted to shed resurge. She yearns for family. For home. But the road leads deep into the mountains, into the split at the heart of herself, through the looking glass to a past she cannot come to terms with. Koliwe/Xolile. Two stories, inextricably linked. Determination to make a difference from now on crystallises in her heart like a gift. Phepile switches on the radio. There are crackles. A radio reporter's moderate tones interrupt Koliwe's thoughts: *This is the BBC World Service...* Her concentration drifts from the headlines, her ears detach from the voice. Clouds form ghostly puffs of breath. Using the window as a pillow, she watches the orange sun sink like a yolk behind the black mountains silhouetted on the horizon.

CHAPTER FOUR

The work canteen reminds her of St Alfred's, with its stewing meat and body smells; the same menu every week; the walls festooned with gurgling, mumbling pipes; tea-coloured blotches staining the ceiling. Crashes and clangs from dropped pans carry from the kitchen. At mealtimes, when employees from other offices pour into the shared refectory, racial divisions re-emerge. Voices clatter in English on one side; on the other, they click in siSwati.

"Ah, it's you," says a deep voice; the man's face partly obscured by a plump woman waiting in line at the catering hatch.

Koliwe slips her glasses on. The face in the queue sharpens.

"Can I help?" Cameron asks.

"Oh, hi." Removing her glasses, Koliwe glances sideways at him.

His lips angle up at the sides; he rests against the catering hatch in beige slacks and a black shirt. They exchange glances. Quickly, he pours a glass of water, and says, "It must be difficult, being new. You won't have made friends yet."

She fills a plate with chicken salad, piles on too much rice and beans. She smooths the dress that hugs her body, finds a tray, fumbles with paper napkins, cutlery; rummages in her bag for money. Her purse zip sticks.

"Allow me." He opens his wallet.

She scans the dining area for an empty table.

"By the window?" he suggests.

There is little room between tables. He has to draw in his stomach, edge around chairs, raise the tray to avoid bumping heads.

The sleeveless dress with slits up both sides flashes her right thigh. She puts her tray on the empty table beneath the window. A poster of King Mswati III hangs on a once white wall stained the yellow of a chain-smoker's fingers. The babble of voices is muffled, as though the canteen is underwater. Seated, she listens intently to Cameron.

"I was scheduled to leave for London last week." He places his plate of braised beef on the table, sits down, and arranges the condiments and cutlery to his satisfaction. "But I was delayed with food transportation for our Mozambican branch." He sighs heavily. "You won't know how long these meetings can be."

Usually she can clean the plate. Today she can only pick at the salad. Her appetite is gone. Warm embers of emotion stir inside her.

"I was discussing plans for next year in a rather gruelling two-day meeting of programme supervisors." He shovels a forkful of meat into his mouth. "My brief includes changing our staff structure." The fragrance of eau de cologne, the resonance of his voice in the room, and that shadow of a Scottish accent, barely discernible, occasionally playing in his words – all this is becoming familiar.

There are no wrinkles on his face. Her forehead rumples like ripples in water. Their eyes meet, then slide away. He is silent while he chews. Who is watching who?

She had a boyfriend before Andrew. Rick, a bright stockbroker with feminine mannerisms and woman's hands. She was crushed when he dumped her, and now he is despised. Who is there for her? Who will keep her in loving arms?

"You understand," Cameron continues, when she looks up, "that while Mr Callow's away, you and I will work closely together." His expression remains firm. "D'you think we'll do okay?"

She replies, "Of course," in a trance-like state.

His tone becomes less formal, almost fatherly. "I always take care of new recruits. Your car, you've collected that?"

She shakes her head.

"Take the Mazda. Start by visiting our four clinics. Claim petrol for field trips, otherwise the car's for your personal use." Sunlight defines the bridge of his nose, catches the two-day stubble on his jaw. "You're finding your way around, aren't you?" he asks.

Koliwe tells him about visiting Thandi.

His eyebrows rise. "Ah, is that so?"

She describes the yard; the shack. Thandi's vulnerability. His eyes cut like a chisel. He follows Koliwe's anecdote as a hound tracks the scent.

"Viewing close up the problems these girls in rural areas tackle can be shocking," he says sympathetically. "Where's home to you?"

Koliwe talks about herself as a small girl. The sensation of drifting through experiences she did not understand, the confused maze of childhood. Weariness engulfs her. From a distance, the past appears clearer, a passion for her work offers the gift of hope.

"D'you know where the Mountain Hotel is?" he interrupts. "There's a conference there a week on Sunday — there'll be a demonstration too. Sipho Matsebula seems hell-bent on disrupting the country. Last time, there was quite a bit of violence. Police used tear gas and live ammunition."

"We'll have to keep our heads down?"

Chuckling, Cameron nods. "This'll be outside your experience, Koliwe."

She fiddles with a napkin. The edges of the largest lettuce leaves on her plate are muddy brown. Examining the withered, unwashed inner leaves, she breathes in deeply to quell the sense of drowning.

"You must present a paper at the conference," he says with conviction.

Dismayed, she shakes her head and reaches for a glass of water.

56

"It'll be good for you."

She picks up the glass, sips from it.

"That's mine," he points out. "I'll get you a drink."

Her hand snatches away from his glass with automatic precision. "No, please." Stiff from tension, weakened; unsteadied, she longs for a straight conversation that isn't stifled and obscure. When she returns with another drink, the table corner smashes into her leg sending shooting pains up her thigh.

His smile is expansive. "I'll be busy the next few days with visitors. I'd like you to take the conference notes, present the paper, then stop off at my house."

She nods evasively at the invitation to his house. She can tell he knows she is too polite to refuse. "What's the conference about?"

"Rural poverty. Please, come visit afterwards. Just before the Swazi Hotel on the left-hand side is a turn-off known as the Tea Road." He pauses. "So named because the English tried to make tea plantations there, and failed." He sketches a diagram on the table, moving the forefingers together. "Drive down the Tea Road until tarmac turns to gravel. Go through the gates, past the gardener's block. There's a long driveway, my house is at the end. You'll see a pool car – the Toyota – in the courtyard." He coolly tips his head back and empties the glass in one swig. "I'll see you a week on Sunday," he repeats reassuringly.

Feeling tired and slightly sick, she heads to the office by way of the stairs, to research the paper. She sees her reflection in the stairwell window and is faced with her inability to say no and the danger that brings.

CHAPTER FIVE

Cameron's L-shaped desk catches the late afternoon sun. Seeking shade, he closes the blinds. He moves without speaking. He looks comfortable; at peace. Koliwe's mornings are long, her lunch breaks short. All afternoon she is lost, her head in her hands amidst a haze of numbers.

Cameron enters the cosy back-office, mumbling something in siSwati. She doesn't understand and doesn't answer. He is taking stock of her loose hair, a mass of frizzy ringlets.

He rests his forearms on her chair back. "Remember, you're gathering information on our pilot projects' successes with improving food production in rural communities." The fabric of his trousers rustles as he shifts his stance. "Boyfriend?" he asks, with an air of detachment.

It is not your place to ask. Her gaze follows the simple print of her knee-length dress, petals of lilac and rusted-pink. His hand brushes the back of her neck. Swift and glittering, something entirely foreign has entered her world and aches with a brooding curiosity. She glances over a shoulder. His hand slips immediately away and he slides out from behind her. Xolile's olive-coloured face; hair, aggressively black, remains imprisoned behind the screen. Koliwe shunts her chair from the corner made by the desk and the filing cabinet, unnerved by the way the body she had has untangled itself. No longer feels her own. She cannot retreat or fade into a dream. Koliwe is on the outside now. She stares back at herself. If she sits very still, Xolile does the same.

A coffee aroma floats through the open doorway, followed by the plip-plonk of Phepile's flat-soled shoes in the corridor.

"Busy?" Phepile lumbers into the back-office, cradling a box of suspension folders. "Breastfeeding programme." She drops the box between Koliwe and Cameron. "Breastfeeding strengthens a baby's immune system." Phepile is as efficient as a photocopier: sorting, stacking, stapling. Her eyes have a reddened tint; bags have formed underneath; years of endurance are written on the dark sagging skin. "Sambulo said she dropped by your place in the hills last week," she is speaking to Cameron. "Said she saw a pretty little thing darting around. Who's that then?" Her pinched lips make a line.

"That's Gift," he replies icily. "My ward. Sometimes she stays with me."

Phepile raises an eyebrow. Cameron grunts and returns to his desk.

Phepile and Koliwe lean over photographs of mothers setting off across misted mountains, their babies tied with blankets to their backs.

"See the tiny ones," Phepile says. "You can hold them." She goes on intuitively, "Xolile, HIV isn't always passed from mother to baby." She has the solid air of a woman who works hard, not only in her salaried job but also at home. She selects a folder from a shelf, flicks through the pages, then writes directions to four HIV clinics. "Visit one a day. Here's the first. Ask Joy Nhlengethwa, the nurse, if she's called on Thandi. A lot can happen in one week."

Scorching sunshine and white scraps of cloud fleck a powder-blue sky. Telephone wires form an overhead grid of cables, a black web of power connecting pylons, stretching into the distance like a troop of tiny skeletal soldiers. The Mazda drives easily. On the passenger seat are Phepile's directions to the first clinic, roughly twenty miles from Mbabane. By mid-afternoon, the mountains are dappled dark blue by drifting cloud. The gentle curves of grassy plains come into view, yellow felt rolled out over a shallow basin. Cattle graze in the great heat.

She crosses a high flat area. Wattle clumps and black thorn bushes border a broad plateau looking down on mountain after mountain. She stops the car, peers through the wattle to a clearing of thatched huts. A woman sits in a doorway; a baby suckles at her breast. Koliwe heads for the shade of roofs, the coolness under the eaves. Cicadas click in the grass; the ardent sun beats down. The mother murmurs and looks up as the child pats her neck. Her silent stare seems friendly.

"Where's the clinic?" Koliwe asks.

She follows the direction of the woman's finger and finds a track through thorn bushes to a concrete block building.

Everything is quiet here, but for the occasional sound of car tyres careering over the yawning potholes that have laid tarmac rugged and raw. Boys patch the weary road with wheelbarrow-loads of stones. Koliwe approaches the gates, a small crowd runs to her, begging. A woman in a nurse's uniform waits in the dusty yard.

"You must be Joy Nhlengethwa?" Koliwe asks.

"And you must be Xolile Dlamini." Joy's smile radiates warmth.

Sunlight pours onto the clinic's corrugated zinc roof. Heat beats up from the baking hot earth and through the soles of Koliwe's sandals to the cushioned balls of her feet. She tramps behind Joy beneath the 'Living Positive' banner strung across the clinic's entrance.

The contrast between the light and dark once through the door leaves Koliwe sightless. Gradually, her eyes adjust. The paintwork in the waiting room has erupted in the heat and spread an eczema-like rash across the walls. Sinewy bodies are sandwiched together on narrow wooden benches, hands clasped between knees. One woman lifts her head: sorrow is sketched on her brow; wrinkled bluish-black skin droops where breasts should be. The testing room has plastic chairs, a wobbly table, boxes of white disposable gloves, sealed test kits, trays of syringes. Steady streams of women come here to test. A smug sense of doing good snuggles in Koliwe's chest.

Joy asks the women probing questions: When did you last have sex? How many partners in the last year? How do you protect yourself? By four o'clock, after the last outpatient has left, Joy and Koliwe step into harsh sunlight.

"Over here we have the infirmary." Joy leads Koliwe through a communal garden strewn with materials for projects that once built hopes – oil drums, the twisted skeleton of a car, deflated inner tubes of tyres. Goats nibble at an aerial sprouting from a truck's bonnet; papaya and mango trees offer solid blocks of shade.

The infirmary is one long room. The smell of death is palpable. Insects, clumps of dirt have fallen from the ceiling. Some inmates lie on the concrete floor wrapped in threadbare bandages, resembling bulky rolled-up rugs. Joy checks blood pressures, pulses, temperatures – dedicated, soldier-like, fortified with the iron will to be undeterred by the conditions in which she works.

Joy's determination is infectious, and while Koliwe silently records the numbers of repeat tests from statistics entered on charts, the desire to do good solidifies in her heart.

"Medical supplies are short," Joy says. "Nothing was delivered last week." She is checking the statistics; long eyelashes shield her eyes. "We have one doctor. He's sick too. Hasn't visited for months. We're giving out condoms, but many men won't wear a condom even when they know they're positive."

Koliwe asks why. Phepile shakes her head.

"How are seriously ill patients treated?"

"We send them home," Joy replies.

"Why?"

"To die."

"And Thandi?"

"Thandi's gone. She was taken away. By a man."

Those who lost the battle for life seem to haunt the sandy yard Koliwe ambles across, on the brick-hard clay path to the gates and her car.

Unsure of the direction, she branches onto a sand track. Sunlight burns her arms, scorches her forehead; white clouds stretch across a watery blue sky. She veers left onto another track, tensed neck muscles cannot relax, sweat-soaked shirt clinging to her back. The track soon gives way to red gravel and grassy patches, then deteriorates into a dirt path leading uphill through scrub.

Already the litre water bottle is empty. Cameron or Phepile should have explained what to bring, exactly what to expect. Her chest is tight with anxiety. To her dismay, the petrol gauge's needle quivers at low. Hoping for directions to Mbabane, she pulls into the wide yard of an isolated homestead of mud and wattle shacks with rusted roofs. It was a mistake. The place looks uninhabited.

As she makes a three-point-turn, sunlight glares bright white on the rear-view mirror, blinding her momentarily. A high-pitched scream slices the air. She looks around guardedly. The leaves on the trees do not stir.

Sensing something moving behind, she wants to swivel round. When she turns her head sharply, whatever she thought she heard or saw is no longer there. More piercing screams split the silence. Someone moves into her peripheral vision. A girl – her dress a bluish streak – is running from one of the shacks.

Waves of fear surge. Something is terribly wrong. Koliwe needs to get out of the car. The girl is crossing stumpy grassland, making a beeline for the Mazda. The top buttons of her dress are undone, the neckline reveals collarbones, a nut-brown shoulder. The girl smashes into the car bonnet. She bangs the windscreen with a fist. They are nose to nose. Close up, the girl's face is blotted with black sunspots. Her skin has a dark bronze tinge. Cheeks, blood-smeared; eyes, filled with anguish. Her mouth is a gaping scream. Every detail holds the evidence of a dreadful happening.

The shack's side door opens. Slams shut. The girl whips around, sprints behind the shack. Koliwe can just make out a man heading after the girl. Koliwe cannot get out of the car, her hands are glued to the steering wheel. Her father whispers: *Don't ever go to Swaziland, they'll eat you alive.* The girl is running full pelt down pitted cattle tracks into tall grasses. The man grabs her hair, yanking her head back. He raises his knobkerrie. There is a clunk as wood hits bone. A streak of panic. Koliwe should be helping the girl, not witnessing the attack. She scans the hills. Distant valleys. The girl has now vanished. With the sun behind him, the man is in silhouette. He turns, wades through the sea of grasses and drops from sight over the valley's lip. Silver clouds shift like shadows across the sky, and yet there is no breezy afternoon coolness. All becomes silent, buried in a sea of grass. Even the wind does not dare to breathe.

Guilt rages through Koliwe. Shaking, she slams the car into gear and begins retracing her route. She shudders at the prospect of having to reason her retreat at a later stage. The engine strains as it rumbles through scrub onto tarmac. The road dips, gently climbs, levels to a wide flat plain.

The sky has grown faintly pink and dusky, the air thick with mosquitoes. She drives across the plateau; the petrol gauge wavers on empty. Cattle are crossing a short stretch ahead; a boy ambles behind them. He is driving the herd to a village, their bony ribcages poke like spokes beneath their hides. She coasts towards the boy, winds the window down, pulls up on the verge. There is the plod of cloven hooves, the pungent aroma of cattle, a whiff of wood smoke here and there.

Lights glimmer ahead in the distance. She snaps, "Which way to Mbabane?" at a boy selling newspapers from a crude clapboard kiosk on the roadside.

He points in the direction she was heading. "It's about thirty centimetres. Takes an hour to drive there."

Coughing and spluttering, the car glides into Mbabane. The light outside the bedsit has faded to nothing. The hall lights flicker, sending an electrical buzz up her spine. Her thoughts go backwards, forwards. Calling an ambulance or going to the police is what she would have done at home.

She thinks of Cameron as she climbs the stairs, mounts the top step, enters the bedsitting room. He is strong. Determined. He said he would take care of her, as though he could light the way. She goes through the arch, perches on the windowsill. Streetlights dim with the depth of night, street noises grow fainter, seeping up to the dark room, the strange bed, through her mind. The city below is dark and ominous.

CHAPTER SIX

The Royal Swazi police headquarters is a grey, austere concrete block.

Phepile trots quickly up the steps. "Reporting the attack will help the police."

Koliwe's explanation to the desk staff is brief. The wait is long. Fresh air enters only when the main doors to the solemn foyer swing open. Guilt multiplies. Intensifies. She should have intervened. Tried to help the girl. The second hand snaps round the wall clock's face; the staccato tick tock marks seconds, minutes, hours of inaction. The hour hand flexes. Eleven. Twelve. One.

Sergeant Lolo's belly stretches the thick material of his uniform to its limits; he has a blood spot in one eye. "Come," he says. Badges parade up the arms of a shirt such a dark blue that it is indistinguishable from black; handcuffs and baton chained to a black duty belt; black tactical trousers with sewn-in truncheon pocket; polished boots. His bald head shines like a coffee bean. This is a man who gives orders. Lolo is as squat and broad as a toad, waddling the narrow corridor to an interrogation room. He crosses the threadbare carpet to another man seated at a desk beneath a one-way glass window.

"My assistant," Sergeant Lolo says.

The assistant is thin, with an angular, rough-shaven face. His uniform is identical to the sergeant's, except his shirt is white. His tiny twinkling eyes slide lazily over Koliwe and up the wall to a portrait of Queen Elizabeth II.

"We can't go on hunches," Lolo says. "We need concrete evidence. Witnesses. Where are you from? Who are you, exactly?"

Lolo's assistant gives Koliwe the hard stare of interrogation.

"I'm from England," she replies. "I work for U.K Aid."

"You must sit," Lolo says. "You saw someone attack someone? Who?"

She shakes her head.

"When did it happen?"

"Yesterday. Monday."

"So, you've hidden evidence from us. Withholding evidence is a punishable offence. Why did you not contact us immediately?"

Another twinge of remorse. "I wanted t-to-o-o be s-sure," she stutters, struck by talons of doubt.

Lolo regards her suspiciously. "Sure of what, exactly?"

"That coming here was right."

"Why would coming here *not* be right?"

Can't they understand? A golden strand of light from the high gleam of day struggles through the long narrow window grille.

The assistant taps a pen against the empty mug beside his computer. He inhales loudly, as though he smells some slip of regret, then looks to the sergeant for consensus.

Lolo rattles the handcuffs clipped to his sturdy leather belt. "You're aware your report can be used as a statement in court. Previous evidence of convictions, such as assault or dishonesty, et cetera, can count against you."

Is she now somehow implicated in the crime? Has she moved from witness to suspect? The air turns cold.

"Something happened... I wish I hadn't driven that far into the mountains." The questioning room walls contract. "It was horrific... a man beat her up."

"Who?" Lolo yelps, disbelief etched on his face. "Can't you answer my question?" the sergeant barks. He drops into the tattered beige seat of his swivel chair, slips a wedge of papers across his desk and, adopting an efficient air, focuses on lists of statistics. "I want to check dates, where you were, where you work," he says softly.

His assistant with the pointed features looks up, bored, and crosses something out in the dog-eared station book.

"Let me describe what I saw." Yet despite the effort of will, her account of the events is stumbling, incoherent and incorrect.

More of the silent paperwork treatment.

"Can a search party be sent out?" she asks.

"Would you recognise him if you saw him again?" the assistant enquires evenly, the suggestion of a smirk curving his lips.

She is uncertain. She crosses her arms on her chest to conceal her quickened breathing, hides her clammy palms beneath her armpits.

"False identification could lead to the long-term imprisonment of an innocent man," adds Sergeant Lolo.

The assistant cocks his thin, bony, bristly face. "What time did this thing happen? Afternoon? Early evening? Night?" He is patient.

"Late afternoon."

"Dusk, hmmm, not much light?"

"It wasn't dusk."

"You were looking into the setting sun?"

"The sun was quite high. Behind them, I think."

Questions come faster now, the interrogators are less patient. While she talks, Lolo's gaze is fixed on her breasts.

"You're sure it really happened? You're not from here, are you? Have you had a reaction to the heat?" There is a snappishness to the assistant's investigations. Without looking at Koliwe, he gets up and leaves the room.

She sighs, wishing she could slide after him beneath the door.

Sergeant Lolo says in a low voice that makes her feel like a stupid child, "Your statement will be filed," then he waddles away.

As she walks to the bedsit, she remembers Arrivals, being carried forward in the confusion; her passport stamped by Swazi officials. Matsapha Airport. The sun was brighter. There was a tumult of colour. Noise. Pushing a trolley laden with cases and bags into Arrivals. Faces waited at the barrier; names scrawled on cardboard. Spotting her placard, hailing Jimmy, the driver, who hauled her luggage into the boot of a four-wheel-drive car. Jimmy had a generous mouth and the cavalier swagger of a man in his early thirties; his belly rolled into pleats as he shifted his overweight body into the driver's seat. He asked, "You don't speak siSwati?" Koliwe dabbed her forehead, fanned her face.

"Do you want a map and some condoms?" a uniformed woman had yelled at the gate in the airport perimeter fence. She drew loops in the air, indicating for the window to be wound down. Koliwe was choked by the question. She said she would just take the map. Then they swept round a fly-over into a labyrinth of concrete curves. Ahead, the scenery was breath-taking – mauve ridged mountains behind rain-specked glass; the lower slopes clothed in pine plantations. Glassy raindrops pierced with sunshine created a crystal chandelier across the blue lakes mirroring the sky. Koliwe's attention had been drawn to a procession of women and men, robed in sombre greys and blacks, scrambling up an embankment. She changed her position, murmuring, "Who are they?"

The driver pulled up to join a line of vehicles on the uneven verge. "You'd best stay here, Sisi." Jimmy melted into the crowds milling around vehicles, huddled against the rain. A deep-rooted discomfort rose within her and she was swayed by waves of fear. But the current of excitement directing her emotions throughout the journey of expectations had left her drained. The crouching tiredness took possession with surprising speed, and she experienced the the isolation of an outsider. The familiar feeling of wanting to run away.

When she awoke, the rain had stopped. Late afternoon sunlight glimmered in the sky and the jam-packed track cleared.

"Why the gathering in the mountains?" she asked, when Jimmy's broad frame appeared.

"Here funerals are, what do you English say... two pennies."

"Two *a penny*, you mean."

"In our culture we say there is no hill without a grave." He added gruffly, "Had to go. She was a friend of mine."

"What did she die from?"

The silence was long and loud. "They'll tell you AIDS, but I know she was murdered."

"How was she murdered? How old was she?"

"It happened in a jealous rage."

She remembers seeing Mbabane that first time, nestled into a green basin backed by the vast wilderness of mountains. The traffic lights switching red to amber, changing the colour of the concrete wall Jimmy parked alongside. She had looked up at a block of flats.

"You're on the third floor," he said.

The entrance was in a narrow passage. Jimmy strained over the luggage in the hall.

She called down from the landing, "Please bring my things up."

"Okay," he shouted back. He waved farewell from the hall where a light shone down from the landing.

Exhausted, she had given a nod of thanks, closed the door.

Now she was swayed by another wave of fear, stronger than the last. Seating herself on the windowsill, she peered through the rusty iron burglar bars.

Headlights glare bright white, eclipsing her sight. She can't draw a blind down to block out the past. The tiniest thing ignites remorse. Draws her into a well of regrets. Shuddering bushes in the park. The shapes of shrubs form the girl's head in profile. Shame and frustration build. She should have pursued the man. Followed the girl's terrible screams.

CHAPTER SEVEN

Humid air, thick with jacaranda scent, climbs with her up the bedsit stairs. The brown paper bag on her doorstep has the dry texture of skin. She switches on the kitchenette light, then withdraws from the bag a heavy fold of cloth. Icy-blue stripes in the material set off the main colour - a deep sumptuous red. Who left the gift?

The evening light has waned. From the bedsit window, shadowy shacks, trees, can just be made out in the park. A car draws up on the far side of the street. The headlights gleam across a mauve carpet of jacaranda blossom. The engine switches off, a window rolls down. A figure hails her from the driver's seat.

"Hey, Xolile!" Cameron yells.

Her body loosens with relief.

"Come down," he shouts up.

Flowers scatter from the pavement, making popping sounds under her feet as she walks in near darkness to his Land Rover.

His cheeks tighten into a smile. "I worry about your safety. Didn't mean to disturb you. Just checking you're okay."

She removes the gold-rimmed glasses and nods, with a slight flutter of her nostrils.

"What's up?" Cameron asks.

The cigarette packet he slams onto the dashboard is scrunched from the tight fit of his pocket. The ends of a scarf peep scarlet above the edges of his collar when he reaches under the packet for a box of matches. He offers her a buckled fag. Lights one for himself.

She studies the rough geography of his face, inhales deeply and, slowly counting to ten, lets out the breath. "There was a man ... in the mountains ... he beat up a girl."

"Dead?"

"I think so. I went to the police."

70

"Ja, police," he barks dismissively. "You've done the right thing."

"They didn't believe me." Agitation spreads through her. "Should I go to the police again?"

"Best not get mixed up in bad business."

"I'm not mixed up." Her hands clench. "There's a duty to . . ."

"Leave it there."

Like a stone dropped into a river, any thoughts of advice sink from reach.

His lips narrow, his eyes widen. His tone is jovial, "I'm sure she'll be found. Local people, with their ear to the ground, truly care about a missing girl." He adjusts the blood-red scarf around his neck to slacken it. "Seen your friend Maureen lately?" he asks, changing the subject.

She shakes her head.

"Saw you two chatting at the colonel's party. Woman's a mess, needs an agent to manage her affairs – financial of course," he guffaws.

"That's what you think of her?"

"She's old fashioned," he says affectionately. "We talk to communicate, but does she have to do it *all the time*?"

Koliwe laughs. "You like her, don't you?"

"Of course I do. But most men don't like Maureen because they know she knows what they're up to." Cameron is leaning into conflict while dancing around it. "I'll disturb you again at some point. I'm your, manager, remember?" He takes a keen drag, then throws the cigarette butt on the pavement and drops into the cab's shadowy interior.

She says she needs to be getting along.

"Quite," he replies.

From the kerb, she watches the Land Rover's red rear lights dissolve into the darkness.

There are two messages on her answer phone. The first, an unfamiliar female voice, leaves a South African phone number. The second, from Cameron, says he has been bartering in Mbabane market, buying colourful batiks to have made into garments. He invites her to stay at his house while he is away on work trips. His tone conveys a mixture of sadness and loneliness. No one else cares about her. Wants her. To share affection should be such a simple thing in life.

She kicks off her sandals, flops into a chair, slides her fingers round the spherical sides of a wine glass. On top of the radio is Cameron's gift of cloth. Although he is not there, he is within reach.

Lights glow from a late-night corner shop. She wants to change whole nations. Wants to better other people's lives. Her wants go deeper than a well. Want. Want. Want. She is so consumed with wanting, she does not notice she has descended the stairs, returned to the bedsit in leaps and bounds, a wine bottle tucked under each arm.

Gunshots reverberate along the street. A vehicle roars away. Quickly, she turns to the window. Peers between burglar bars. Dark windows are mirrors. She makes a tunnel with her hands either side of her face. A solitary figure slides from the alley. She drops onto the settee. Pours glass after glass. To fill the hollow within. A breath of air wafts across her cheek. She is haunted by a feeling of being watched in an otherwise empty room.

She brushes aside strands of hair clinging to her neck. And feels utterly lost. She is with no one. Not even herself. Xolile.

CHAPTER EIGHT

Late morning, there is knocking at the door. Who might visit on a Saturday? Who knows her address?

A short, plump woman stands on the landing. Her hair is cropped close, her complexion mahogany-brown. The podgy cheeks and bridge of her nose are slightly pocked and sprinkled with paprika-coloured freckles.

"Where's Xolile?" she asks abruptly. A plum-coloured shawl decorated with pictures of King Mswati III is draped over her well-built shoulders; a firm knot on her ample bosom holds the shawl in place. Her violet dress has small red dots in the print; beads of moisture stand out on her puffy neck and forehead. Koliwe has never seen the woman before, but the curve of her brow, the way her lips reveal a broad gap between her front teeth, is vaguely familiar.

The woman says, "I look for Xolile. Is your name Koliwe or Xolile?" She offers a clammy hand. "You know who I am?" Her smile is contagious.

All the same, Koliwe clings to the door handle.

"I'm Rachel Mhlanga. I am your aunt, Xolile." The woman throws her arms wide.

A rope has been thrown across the chasm – there, on the landing – but Koliwe hangs back. "Why didn't you answer my letter?"

Rachel shakes her by the shoulders. "Look at you!"

"Dad never said much about you." Stepping backwards, Koliwe remembers what he had said: *Superstitious woman, devoted to ancestor worship and rituals.*

"Why did he never write or phone to tell *me* about *you*, Xolile?" Pulling their bodies together again, Rachel presses Koliwe's head between her breasts in a suffocating, back-slapping, hug. "I don't know where to start." Rachel's hearty belly laugh seems to shake the block. "You and me, we've plenty of time for talking." She releases her grip – just in time for air.

The hall lights buzz and flicker. Rachel waltzes into the kitchenette and through the arch to the bedsitting area. Koliwe follows; her father, the artist, a shadow in her mind, as she tries to unravel her family history and weave it into a picture that makes sense. Beaming broadly, talking excitedly, Rachel admires the eggshell-blue colour of the linoleum and remarks upon the scant furniture.

Koliwe wonders what is expected of her. Joy and confusion bubble up in equal measures. "How did you find me?" she asks.

"Mbabane's not large. People talk," Rachel says, with a shrug. She pokes the Russian dolls out of line on top of the ply-board dressing table. The largest doll is stoic; four of the smaller dolls fall down. The tiniest topples over the edge and rocks rhythmically from side to side on the floor. Nothing, not even this mishap, wipes the smile from Rachel's face.

Crouching, Koliwe cradles the tiniest doll, a solid chunk of wood, in her palm. She swivels the tops from the wooden dolls to place the innermost baby within the bellies of its five mothers. Xolile is covered in sleep. She awakes. Listening.

As Koliwe stands, the prickly unease since Rachel appeared becomes impossible to ignore. "How did you know I was *here*?"

"Cameron."

"You know Cameron? My boss?"

"Oh yes." Rachel chortles. "But I don't live in Swaziland. Like your father, I left. I'm living in Joburg, working freelance for the Ministry of Tourism. You must come and stay, Xolile. And what about your mother? She must be…"

"Have a seat." Koliwe uses the wall as a prop.

"Coming from England, you won't know much about our national customs," Rachel continues, settling into cushions. "Usually, the wife of the deceased would remarry into the family – because of the lobola," she explains.

Koliwe glances round the sparsely furnished bedsit. Mum wouldn't have settled here – the cracked lino, the black imitation leather settee, cheap wardrobe, rust-encrusted mirror, Matryoshka smiling sweetly on the dressing table. She says bluntly, "Mum's dead."

"Ah." Rachel's smile evaporates. "Oh, I'm so, so sorry."

"Cancer. I was twelve."

"You must say if you need anything, *anything*, eh." Rachel forages in her handbag for cigarettes and a lighter, then clasps a cigarette between finger and thumb as though it is a wand and she has transformed into the fairy godmother. "Sit down – no, stand up. How old is my only England niece, eh? Let me look at you better."

Sheepishly, Koliwe stands to attention. "I'm twenty-three."

Sucking nicotine in, "Oh," Rachel sighs effusively, "oh, that is good."

Hurriedly, Koliwe fetches a glass of water and an ashtray. Supressed memories surface. That miserable grey day; the coffin encasing her mother. The church bells' peal across a crowded cemetery. The back of her hand catches a falling tear.

Rachel burrows her bottom into cushions like a hen in a dust-bath, shaking off the heat. "Please don't be upset," she clucks, reaching out. Her handbag tips over; credit cards, purses, wads of tissues, crinkled slips of paper, a Zippo lighter, keys, cascade across the floor. She nudges the chaos with a foot riddled with varicose veins bulging between dainty gold sandal straps, and picks out a handkerchief with which to dab her pudgy face. "*Lord*, to think I'll never ever see my brother, Moses, again."

Koliwe grieves for Xolile. For the Swazi family she has yet to meet.

Little wrinkles form on Rachel's brow. She seems to be searching for words. "Moses, your father," she pats the cushions for Koliwe to sit beside her, "he was the naughty one. He went to England when I was twelve. He must have been eighteen, but he stayed, isn't it?"

Koliwe recites the story. "Dad was the eldest son, your parents sold most of their cattle to send him to university. They held high hopes for their English-educated son qualifying as a doctor or lawyer and returning to run their small farm. But he stayed in the mother country." Which, she recalls, accounted in part for his depression. The shame of unemployment accounted for his dolefulness.

Rachel claps a hand around Koliwe's shoulder. "You're looking worried," she says, fanning her face with her own hand.

That last evening at the cottage with her father, sunlight glowed through the study window, casting amber streaks across his hair. Cigarette ends floated in a brandy glass on the seat of his wicker chair. Koliwe hated seeing him drunk. His skies, an ashen wash, were too dark for the time of year. Paint trickled like tears down the canvas, smearing the low Chiltern hills. She bristled as she went to his side, and upset his brandy. Dappled in sunlight, dappled in silence, her father had no one to turn to but her. She had no one to turn to but him.

What to say about his years of alcohol-induced stupor? The pills he had knocked back as if they were candy?

Rachel's eyes shine with adoration, or naiveté. Ferreting through her handbag, she says, "I only have this picture," and hands over a black and white photograph crinkled, yellowed with age, of two children, side by side on a bench. The girl wears a frock. The boy, shorts, ankle socks, hands splayed over his knees; hair cut close to the shape of his small oval head. He could be anyone.

"That's me." Tears well in Rachel's eyes. Her hand floats over the girl, grasping at shadows of her past. "Hey, I was seven... That's... forty-three, no, forty-five years ago. Only two of us survived. Me and Moses."

Already the humidity is high. Columns of sunlight streak the room, creating a drowsy atmosphere. Moses, facing his daughter, shimmers in the white glare from the window. Glowering at a life's work – failed expectations: thickly painted oils; broad energetic strokes. The colours are at first strident – as he becomes more desperate, more unhappy, bleed into monotone. Gripped by self-destruction, he paints his home country in apocalyptic shades.

The weight of loss makes Koliwe buckle into the settee; head bowed, tears stream down her face. Silently, she ruminates. How to reach out from heart-wrenching sorrow?

"Some people want to forget their past." Rachel has assumed a motherly tone. "There would have been a calling, bringing his spirit back home. *Lord,* I have lost my only brother," she wails. She sucks in her cheeks, wipes tears from eyes, bulbous from crying. "Everyone has to go... but it's all wrong," she sniffles. "Moses, drowned?"

Koliwe refocuses, scrutinizing the blurred photograph. A shutter has opened on a moment from her father's childhood.

"Something's bad, I smell it. There's something you're not telling," Rachel concludes, scratching her leg.

For the next half hour, Rachel broods, asks questions, digs suspiciously into the past, intent on extracting incriminating information. Koliwe offers cups of tea.

From her bag, Rachel produces two tiny packets of biscuits. "Tea and biscuits, like you have in England," she exclaims, popping chocolate Bourbons into her mouth. "Why, if Moses and you lived by a river, didn't he learn to swim?"

Exasperated, Koliwe sighs. "It's not right to search for someone to blame." She turns to her aunt. When their eyes meet, Rachel's gleam haughtily.

Koliwe watches her aunt's hands rotate in her lap. Rachel stares at one palm then the other, comparing them as though alternating emotions of intense love and hate draw her in opposite directions. Rachel holds an ambivalence towards her brother that Xolile understands.

"You're as stubborn as your father," Rachel says under her breath. Her voice wavers, as though her feelings have been hurt. "It's always the same." She flops back into the settee. Again, her eyes seek Koliwe's. The look is dark, very far off.

Koliwe sees her father in Rachel's face and knows she isn't lying. Silence descends upon the room. Koliwe passes the photograph back.

Rachel smokes two cigarettes to the filter tip, hastily stubs them out, then rakes the clutter back into her handbag, shakes the whole lot down and rises. She goes through the archway and heads for the front door with an air of determination.

"You're leaving already?" Koliwe asks.

Rachel pauses: the shawl slips round to reveal the low cut back of her dress. The violet cloth compliments her purple-brown skin, where strong sunlight has caught the nape of her neck and her muscular shoulders. She wheels round – her movements fluid despite her bulky body – and, with a tissue, swabs her forehead and the bridge of her nose. "We know Moses died in a river. Was he pushed, did he fall in, or what?" She is heading once more for the settee.

"He drowned."

"You haven't answered my question."

Koliwe wishes she knew the answer. She is back there searching for him, hurrying down the riverbank through the silver-grey mist of a light shower. Clutching at reeds, throttled by fear. The post-mortem said her father's blood was full of alcohol. Cause of death, drowning. Misadventure or possible suicide.

But Rachel is the sort of woman who gets what she wants. She dumps her ample bottom onto the settee. Her heavy breasts rise; fall. "I have the notion none of this was accidental." She exhales loudly and reclines deeper into cushions. "Because of the way Moses passed, it was uncomfortable for a lot of people. Xolile, he should be returned to his ancestral home."

Koliwe's voice wavers. "England is where he lived."

"Swaziland is where he was born." With a note of satisfaction, Rachel adds, "Moses included me in his will."

Koliwe replies, "Yes, that was strange. He hadn't been in touch with family here for years."

"He left a generous sum, enough to buy..."

"He was depressed," Koliwe replies dismissively. "His state of mind impaired his ability to reason."

Rachel nods before speaking again. "At least you've got the right name."

"What do you mean?"

"Xolile, in siSwati, names have a meaning. Yours, Xolile, means 'One Who Forgives'. Moses," she pauses, "when we heard of his death... The way it happened is what we don't accept."

"What? Why?"

Rachel's look becomes menacing. "It must have been accidental, mistaken as suicide."

Certain her aunt has not seen the post-mortem, Koliwe shifts her weight, guilt snakes through her insides. Has she humiliated her aunt by saying or doing something terrible? She is lost on a plane of betrayal. Guilt. Shame. Had her scream caused her father to fall? "Why keep asking about this?"

"When a person dies, the scenes here would be quite unbelievable, for you," continues her aunt, crossing stumpy legs. "There's a way to grieve – a right way to do it. Here, people express their grief vocally. Is that the word, vocally? Wailing, fainting. Family members and friends come to pay their respects day after day, ending in a night vigil. Men aren't entirely tearless, also. Yet emotion is frowned upon in the U.K, isn't it?"

At both her parents' funerals, Koliwe had been grief-stricken. Crazed. Her body flickering with agony. Tears prickle, her vision blurs. Outside, trees lean, quiver; the mauve and purple mountains' faces are split with crevices. A sunbird shrieks mournfully. Despite the fault, the shame, she maintains a matter-of-fact tone: "What do you want from me?"

"Tell me, was there a night vigil? No? There should've been a night vigil." Then Rachel says decisively, "He's not at rest. A restless spirit, a living ghost." Throwing up her hands, she raises her voice, "He *cannot* rest! He is yearning to be with the ancestors!"

Koliwe collapses back into cushions. Xolile touches the wetness on her cheek.

Then Rachel's demeanour changes. Trying a different, calmer tack, she settles deeper into the seat. "Was he cremated?"

Koliwe can't talk about this either. She folds her arms across the chest of her tear-soaked shirt. Koliwe and Xolile. One half crumbling; the other half brick-hard.

"You've been to see a sangoma?" There is anxious inquiry in Rachel's eyes. "Perhaps you should visit a sangoma. A seer. The sangoma's methods can work better than Christianity and the South African doctors in Mbabane. They might tell you to find a white hen or cockerel, slaughter it and cleanse yourself with the blood. Thirty days after a man's burial there's usually a cleansing ceremony for the family's women, you see."

Koliwe shakes her head. Is this woman nuts?

Rachel's expression is fixed, her voice flares with determination. "Moses *should've* been buried in his ancestral home. His mother's mother, his gogo, that's your great-grandmother, was a princess—"

"He never said we were related to the *king!*" A life unknown to Koliwe is going on around her. A life that is hers, but one of which she has no experience. No understanding. Here, Xolile belongs.

"But," continues Rachel, "there would've been some problem-making – is that the right word? – about whether he should be buried, and if so, where. The elders would know whether the body should be buried in the Sibaya or placed in a cave. You see, women are buried in the ground. If a man kills himself" – her voice sharpens with scorn – "he might be buried with the women. Usually, you go to the site of their death and chant, and collect a little bit of soil or a reed pipe, isn't it, then burn it or bury it."

"Where, in a cave?" Koliwe asks.

"The burial place of Dlamini is at Mdzimba, the long mountain near Manzini. It's a sacred royal burial site, you can't visit."

Rachel's hand moves onto Koliwe's arm. In her aunt's eyes is a brown distant look. For a fleeting moment, Koliwe is with her father. There is the grandfather clock's pendulum swinging; the whisky aroma, a balance of almond, honey, peat. His life is a series of paradoxes. Moving from Swaziland's rural poverty to the whiteness of Oxfordshire. His union with her mother – the forbidden fruit. His anchor. With her, he was tougher than teak. Her mother's death changed him. Too much to reconcile. No wonder he does not rest.

"Ancestors are consulted – consulted, is that the right word? – throughout the mourning period," Rachel explains. "They're a constant presence, you mustn't battle with them. You can't commit him to God."

Koliwe feels a part of herself she could not know then. Xolile.

Rachel is watching a line of ants crawl across the floor. "Kute lidloli lelayekela kabo," she murmurs.

At a loss, Koliwe looks to her aunt questioningly.

"Spirits want to return home, isn't it, Xolile?"

Koliwe cannot answer.

Rachel sponges tears from her own cheeks with a sleeve. "You may experience a catalogue of disasters, Xolile. This will be from the ancestors." Rachel's posture is composed, her delivery measured, as though she is reading from an instruction manual. "Because Moses wasn't buried in the right place, someone might die in an untimely way – an accident, or a murder. Slaughtering a beast could appease the ancestors, but for someone who hasn't maintained the family connection, it's very difficult, hei."

"What do you mean?" Koliwe has that rollercoaster lurch she has when driving too fast over a humpback bridge. Rachel holds diametrically opposed beliefs, speaks a different language, yet hails from the same family.

Rachel nudges her elbow into Koliwe's ribs. "Eh, you understand me, eh?"

"You mean being buried away from his birthplace has made Dad's spirit uneasy?"

"That's what I'm saying one-hundred percent," Rachel purrs. "What's wrong?" she asks. "You're hurting, I see it in your body."

Above the highest trees, behind the flats, are the slanted sides of mountains. They look insurmountable.

"Don't blame yourself," Rachel says.

In this moment there is only the rushing river. The earthy aroma of sheep. Back in her treasured place – a leafy hollow, tree trunks are speckled with flickering light. Her mind wanders wildly across the river. Elusive sunlight. Clouds skate on the surface. Beneath, lies her father.

"Moses is telling us something must be done," Rachel says firmly. "I'll tell the family what's been happening. They'll know what to do. The rest will be up to them. The elders may arrange a ceremony, the slaughter of a goat, or cattle, to appease our ancestors. They'll explain the troubles you're having."

Too tired to object, Koliwe focuses on the mountains. Trees blur and darken. Rachel is not the wise woman Koliwe had hoped for. Irritation with her aunt mingles with anger.

Rachel's head is wagging. "My child, *Lord*, oh my child, this is what I feared." She holds Koliwe to her cushiony breasts, to skin sticky as honey, and the synthetic violet fabric of her dress. She pats Koliwe's cheeks, clamps them between hot clammy palms and lifts and kisses both sides of her face. "I'll deal with this. Tomorrow, I leave for Joburg. As soon as I'm back here, I'll phone."

Koliwe says forcefully, "Please, don't leave."

Rachel is already through the archway; the heels of her sandals clack-clatter on the vinyl.

Disappointed, Koliwe slumps against the doorframe.

Rachel swivels round. "Xolile." She is poised on the landing, her face glistening with sweat. "I'll pray to the ancestors for you." Hastily she descends the stairs.

Koliwe sinks into the warm impression her aunt left on the settee, then shifts to one side and finds Rachel's half-empty cigarette packet beneath a cushion. She gets up, checks the door is locked and windows are secured. The face in the bathroom looking-glass has a mask-like quality. One half bathed in sunlight with a coppery sheen. She tucks russet ringlets behind her ears. Glass reflects the tarnished glitter of hope, golden-olive cheekbones. The other half, in shadow, has midnight undertones; black curls glisten like oiled ebony. There was the sense of unbelonging in England. In Swaziland, her Englishness sets her apart. The unknown felt part struggles to emerge. One face. Two names. Koliwe. Xolile.

CHAPTER NINE

She strolls past stall after stall selling lucky beads, porcupine quills, necklaces. The sky is stained copper-mauve; the warm air sweet. The low walls of Mbabane marketplace are cracked and dented with the pockmarks of bullets, scars of decay. Shutters hang loosely from rusted hinges. Trucks swish past carrying elderly men with weathered skin. Girls walk hand in hand, their faces brim with laughter – one has prominent cheeks; the other a wide forehead and a dimpled chin. Their reflections skate across Koliwe's in the supermarket window. Weighed down with bags of provisions, she enters the narrow pedestrian underpass from the supermarket. The ceiling is low, the light gloaming at the end. Two youths are in a scuffle ahead; their voices, the thud of their footfall reverberates against the concrete walls. Koliwe keeps to one side, but the youths hurtle into her, shoving her into the middle.

A woman appears from nowhere. She yanks Koliwe backwards, shouting fiercely at the boys. Re-gaining her balance, breathless, Koliwe puts down her carrier bags.

"You must watch out." The woman slouches against the wall. It is nearly dark and the tired colour of her skin, fleshy-pink like mushrooms, merges with the pearly-greyness of the underpass. "New here?"

"Not exactly. Maureen, isn't it?" Koliwe puts out her hand. "We met at the colonel's party."

"I call him the Old Colonial," Maureen replies with a titter. "You're Xolile?"

"And you're Maureen."

Maureen looks embarrassed. She is shorter than Koliwe. Maureen pulls a fistful of greasy notes from her jeans back pocket and, grinning tentatively, shoves them back as she delves for pencil and paper from her other pocket. "I'm waiting for a friend, but she's usually late. Here." She scribbles something on

84

the wrinkled paper scrap. "My address, in case you need it." She swipes blonde strands of hair from her forehead.

Koliwe folds the scrap into a neat square.

Maureen drops back into semi-darkness; her features indistinct, dominated by shadowy patches on the wall. "British Aid's Project Coordinator, aren't you?"

"No, I'm the D.O."

"D.O?"

"Development Officer."

"Of course, I'd forgotten. How's it going?"

Koliwe shrugs. It is her prerogative not to explain. Maureen lights a cigarette. The flare from the match illuminates her face; when she inhales, the tip glows orange-red through the blackness. "Like to join me for drinks sometime?"

They move on together, the plastic bags cutting into Koliwe's hands. The beat of their footfall, thrown back by the walls, echoes then fades.

"I hear you'll be at Sunday's conference," Maureen says.

Koliwe wonders how she knows, as Maureen talks on. Maureen spent her early childhood in India, now works as an English teacher, teaching Swazi children to read. As they approach the entrance, the echoes recede. Their voices, their footsteps, become dull sounds.

Maureen swivels round. She half-asks, half-states in the murkiness of twilight, "I'll see you then."

After Maureen turns the street corner, Koliwe, surrounded by shadows, cigarette smoke, bags of shopping, fishes Maureen's address from her pocket, scrunches the paper scrap into a minute ball and flicks the ball into the gutter. Then picks it out, unfolds it, reads the spidery scrawl and plops it in a shopping bag.

For the end of November, it is dry, the temperature is high for early morning and the swallows' wings sweep across a still blue sky. The conference is to start at ten. It is nine thirty-five when Koliwe swings the Mazda onto the Mountain Hotel's forecourt.

An army of lean men, dressed in factory overalls or like farm labourers , is flocking around the parking area. Ten or more are assembling a rostrum from pineapple pallets. She manoeuvres her car into an empty parking space. A car park attendant lunges at a demonstrator, twisting the man's arm behind his back. She recalls, as she glimpses the man writhing and squirming, Cameron had said there might be trouble, a demonstration. In the same instant she spots Cameron himself.

Majestic white columns set on a plinth frame the hotel's palatial doorway. The neo-classical face of the building has recently been whitewashed; an ostentatious balcony protrudes over the red carpet, which ascends a flight of stone steps to a revolving door. Cameron shouts something from the top step, but the rallying cries from the masses gathered drown his words.

"Wait," she calls, hastening her stride. She reaches the red carpet and gains steps two at a time.

Cameron bows his head in greeting. "That's Sipho." He points out a muscular man in his middle years sauntering across the forecourt.

Sipho is easily recognisable, in a scarlet T-shirt and black jeans, as the demonstrator she saw worming himself free of the official. Sipho has smoothly moulded features; his eyes glower – a rebellious look; his hair, a series of spiky clumps, looks coarser than sugar cane. He carries a megaphone and swings his arms as he moves through the restless mob. Mounting the top step, satchel slung over her shoulder, Koliwe is preoccupied with steering clear of the demonstration. She shoots Sipho a cursory glance and then plunges through the revolving door.

The hotel's ritzy four-star décor of crimson and bronze contrasts strikingly. The foyer is crowded with government officials, aid workers, diplomats, who all stand a few inches taller than her.

Cameron's sombre grey suit has a slight sheen. He looks sharply down his hawkish nose. His attaché case nudges her shin.

"Do you" – she has been wondering – "ever stop to give locals a lift in your car? Is it safe?"

"Swazi, if they miss a bus, are content to wait a day or two," he says, curling his lip acrimoniously.

He slides his case onto the reception desk. He opens the lock, flicks back the catches, discreetly shuffles papers inside. His cheeks dimple; he has slipped back into his charming self.

Koliwe takes a pen and pad of paper from her satchel, then leafs through her conference pack.

Sipho launches through the revolving door. Close up, Sipho is not pretty. His face is shiny with sweat; his forehead curves down to a bulbous nose; a tumorous growth from a knife slash scars his left cheek. He twists his upper lip crudely at Koliwe. The privileged expatriate bitten by guilt. She is distracted by a loud roar of protestation from the demonstrators outside. Cameron straightens up. He gives Sipho the cold glare. Coolness spews through the foyer with a mechanical whir of air-conditioning.

"Don't have anything to do with Sipho, or any other union members, for that matter," Cameron mutters, turning from Sipho, taking Koliwe's arm. There is a whiff of aftershave – sandalwood spiked with cardamom; a match is struck, igniting that spark inside her again. "Lunch is provided here, thank God. I'll see you at my house after the conference."

She disappears to the washrooms. The granite floor sparkles with silver specks. Tea candles and fake lotus flowers float in the washbasins; the whiteness of hand towels, the luxury vanilla moisturiser, heightens the sense and the sanitised scent of European success.

She studies the hotel noticeboard as the foyer fills. Presently, a steward opens the double doors of the main conference hall to reveal the panoramic view behind the podium. Seated, she pins her name tag to her dress, then gazes out of the window. Serried rocky ranges form the backdrop, their rugged tops flushed with sun. Mountains, known as Sheba's Breasts – exuberant, twin-peaked – shimmer misty-grey in the middle-distance, towering over an indigo plain. The forest in the foreground spreads a pine green eiderdown.

Delegates arrive throughout the opening address. All the chairs have been taken by the end of the keynote speech. The first paper presented for discussion is 'To Eradicate Poverty and Recover with Dignity'. Agitated, fretful on the podium, the speaker rolls his weight from one leg to the other. "The faces of abject poverty are many. Loss of human dignity. Denial of opportunities. Poverty is not just about low incomes. Inextricably linked to the legacy of apartheid…" he drones on.

The delegates busily take notes; a battalion of heads bobs up and down. Someone drops their papers. Sunlight streams from a high window in thick golden shafts.

An aroma of fresh coffee wafts into the hall, delegates clear the rows of chairs. The break was well-timed.

Koliwe joins a fast-moving line behind a slender woman in a lightweight emerald suit. Recognisable as the person who had 'rescued' Koliwe from the thugs. Her ash-blonde hair is styled up into a classic bun, her slender neck gives an elegant appearance, the black onyx necklace and matching drop earrings set off her milky-white skin. The woman's name tag reads: Maureen Dlamini. How strange, she and Maureen share the same clan.

Maureen skilfully rests her conference pack across her forearm as a table for her cup. "No doubt you've heard Sipho appealing to the prejudices of the mob, and British aid workers coming out with loads of guilt about famine and aid?" She sips at her steaming coffee, her dismissive tone at odds with her immaculate appearance, "They're all constipated, Koliwe, full of shite." On tip-toe now, peeping over the tops of heads, Maureen speaks about life as she sees it. "For new arrivals like you, there's very little here." She adds, "I'm not English.

I'm from the Scottish Borders, near Galashiels. Look, there's Cameron." Maureen smooths her ash blonde hair neatly behind her ears and squints beyond him at the mountainous scenery. "I once knew your boss rather well. Have you two become close?" She laughs naughtily. "Play your cards right and..."

Koliwe returns a polite smile, but that is the end of the exchange.

The conference resumes. From her seat at the back of the hall, Koliwe absorbs debates on methods for reducing rural poverty and conscientiously makes notes.

The chair announces, "Our next speaker, Xolile Dlamini."

Koliwe mounts the podium, shoulders squared. "In the light of advancing feminist trends, plentiful funds must be available for women's projects." She is braced like a deer who, when startled, bounds into the glen. She stresses the necessity for a socio-economic approach when implementing change. "What I learned from a western education doesn't address the real issues. We at U.K Aid appreciate the complexities of the nation's challenges. U.K Aid is building on its reputation of helping child-headed families." Cameron watches, hawk-like. Emotions are physical sensations coursing her body.

There is muted applause. The smell of food becomes visible.

Delegates descend to the lower ground floor to feed on veal canapés and game terrine. Men in safari suits. Men with hefty salaries – all talking tenaciously, while white women in shot silk or crepe dresses bustle and fuss around them. The lunch menu is extravagant. Tables groan with silver platters of chicken and lamb skewers, finely sliced honey-roast ham, braised beef, green beans, cauliflower in anchovy sauce, rum-soaked apples, chocolate gateaux topped with glacé cherries, lemon cheesecake, mango mousse. Thandi's yard flashes before Koliwe's eyes. The shack of mud, wattle, corrugated metal.

Cameron tries to catch her on the stairs. She ducks behind a rock-water feature with Romanesque trailing plants. Phepile and her three other office colleagues turn from Koliwe coldly, critically, on account of her speech. On her way from the eatery, she is sandwiched between a Corinthian column and a man with menacingly blue eyes and a handlebar moustache. In this corner of the world garden, they all look mysteriously at home.

Jeanette, accoutred with thick, oily makeup, her hair restyled into a pixie cut since Colonel Johnston's dinner party, approaches with a loaded plate, hailing Koliwe cheerily with a raised fish fork. "Ah, Koliwe, how are they treating you at that Aid office now? Showing you the sights?" Jeanette is sweating and her warpaint runs. She adds, "They always do us proud at this hotel. It's been well worth us flying from Ethiopia – the conference agenda's so... so relevant to my husband's work."

Coffee, mints and more declarations are digested. The seating in the conference hall moves for a range of workshops and discussions on the effects of HIV on poverty-stricken rural communities. Lazy sunlight specked with dust motes slices the room in two. Targets are set, decisions made. Satisfaction floats down from lofty altitudes.

A motion is passed to hold a conference on the same issues next year.

She squeezes through the crowd of departing delegates, but at the revolving door stops short. The mob on the forecourt has swollen to several hundred. A thick mass of demonstrators is congregating on the far side of the main road, a steady stream flows across the central reservation. Angry eyes gleaming, they flood onto the forecourt, each looks intent on causing trouble. The pineapple pallets are being dragged away by troops of uniformed stewards, and now the mass is advancing on the hotel, jeering, chanting, protesting.

Aid workers swarm at the revolving door like bees around honey. Tentatively, some make their way down to the car park. Koliwe falters on the top step, then descends. Soon she is immersed in the multitude, trapped between aid workers and jostling protesters holding up placards advertising the Independent Swaziland Party. Cameron has vanished. Swazi flags are being raised – and there is Sipho's broad forehead, his unkempt hair, strong face, defining scar. Scanning the forecourt, she glimpses a bright sliver of green. Maureen's suit. Head down, Maureen edges through a dense thicket of angry men. Shoulder to shoulder, the crowd hums and bristles. It is fast becoming a riot. Taking a deep breath, Koliwe elbows through the crush. The rank sweaty stench is stifling. She catches sight of Jeanette – a shock of ginger hair. Fear flickers across Jeanette's face; her voice leaks through the din: "Get out, darling, quick as you can!"

Sipho, his feet grounded squarely on the one remaining wooden pallet, stands higher than his supporters, bystanders and uniformed hotel stewards. Brilliant sunshine bleeds through bleached clouds, crowning him with lucent yellow. Koliwe forces herself into the body of the crowd. She is shocked by the violent din, half-suffocated from lack of air, hemmed in by bare raised arms. A sinister convoy of black SUVs ploughs through the multitude, the delegates cloistered behind tinted heat-reflective glass. Men hoisting placards declaring *We Want Pay Rise* and *Strike Out Competition* cry slogans at the tops of their voices.

"Swaziland is not poor," Sipho shouts into the megaphone, pronouncing each word with precision. The mob in front quietens. "The British and South Africans are not poor," his voice booms. "The King is not poor. The aid workers are not poor. It is only us, the Swazi population, who are poor."

Cheers rise and whistles pierce the air. Koliwe bursts from the demonstration and into sunlight again.

CHAPTER TEN

Pavements on the edge of town are lined with agitators. Koliwe drives down the mountainside, turns off at the Tea Road, and the air becomes quiet, but even away from the noise and the clamour, her heart races.

A fence of diamond-shaped mesh with a top strand of razor wire demarcates the outer limits to the compound of Cameron's house. She recognises the wrought-iron gates from his description and continues between trim flowerbeds and neat green lawns. A semi-circle of ornamental trees defines a pond on one side; on the other, a low fence marks the boundary of a small bungalow. This, she assumes, is the gardener's quarters. It has its own vegetable plot, a fair-sized lawn and a flourish of flame trees.

The drive continues through open gardens to another set of gates. A bungalow stands on the far side. Compared to her bedsit, Cameron's property is sublime. A rockery planted with flowering shrubs and orange and mauve striped lilies is central to a courtyard paved with granite slabs. She spots Cameron through the gates' ornate ironwork, crouched over a box of tools in front of a double garage. There is a fluttering in her stomach. She is surprised he is busying himself about the house so soon after the conference.

Two Alsatians dart across the courtyard, snarling and snapping. She stops the car. Cameron looks up, waves her on. But the gates are bolted. Perspiration dribbles down the small of her back. The noise, the chaos from the demonstration earlier, and, contrastingly, seeing Cameron in these homely surroundings, sets her on edge. She gets out of the car once he has called the dogs.

He shades his eyes from the sun. "You found it all right?" He strolls to the gates.

"Yes, I had no trouble." Leaning against the car door, she is partially dazzled by the glare of the whitewashed walls. "I haven't seen a demonstration like that before," she admits.

"I warned you there'd be a disturbance."

The fruity scent of ripe pineapples carries from fields in the Malkerns Valley and mingles with the perfume rising from lilies in the rockery. The pungent aromas, the humidity, the demonstration — distant and unruly — all give the present a harrowing sharpness.

"How did you get back so quickly?" she asks timidly.

"I left early, immediately after lunch," he explains. "Something happened?"

Coming closer to the gates, she speaks in a small voice, "How long have you lived here?" She feels she is trespassing on forbidden land. A strained silence ensues. She smooths wispy curls back from her face. "It's really a beautiful place."

"The grounds are fenced off by stock wire." He gestures around the courtyard. "This is where the dogs spend most of their time. There's enough space for them to wander, but Nathi, the gardener, takes them for a walk whenever he can." He opens the gates. The dogs rush out and, to divert them, he lobs a tennis ball as far as he can across the lawns. "There are trees beyond the fence, so if you're coming here at night, Koliwe, it may be very dark. I hire a guard from a local firm, he runs to open the gates when I arrive. Electric gates would be the answer."

"What are the dogs called?"

He laughs. "They're not pets. They don't have names — just guard dogs with a job to do."

Her confusion and attraction for him makes the air dense and strange. Breathe deeply, she tells herself. Relax. "The conference was more interesting than I'd expected. I made notes." She eyes the Alsatians romping in the gardens. "And I bumped into that woman, Maureen."

93

A bothered look crosses Cameron's face. He strolls in the direction of the double garage, where there is a kennel and blankets for the dogs. A uniformed guard sits on the kennel, staring dully.

She treads warily, pretending to know less than she does. "Have you met someone called Rachel Mhlanga?"

"It's a small community. People know each other." Cameron squats by his collection of tools and inspects the garage door. The door is compressed in folds. He reaches up, and raises and lowers the handle; the repeated levering action releases the catch slotting into the rail.

"Rachel lives in South Africa. Maureen was at the conference and," she hesitates, then dares to let curiosity get the better of her, "she asked about you."

Cameron becomes still and the guard stares dully at him. Expectation moulds her expression. All she has is a view of his back. He glares over his shoulder; his lean countenance leather-hard; beads of sweat glimmer on his skin. Then, immediately, his sight reverts to the rail.

"The guard sits in the garage, but patrols around quite often," he announces. "He's quiet. Serious. Doesn't sleep on the job. We have the night guard too. He is very sharp. He's going to be good." He rises with a tenseness about him. He clasps the door handle and, with his spine as rigid as a tin soldier's, walks half the length of the garage, sliding the door behind him. He has left the guard in virtual darkness.

The larger Alsatian charges across the lawn, the ball in his mouth. The other dog gambols against him; their hackles rise when they reach the courtyard gates. Koliwe cringes. The dogs are baring fangs and growling.

"You're quite safe as long as I'm here," Cameron says. He snaps his fingers to bring the dogs to heel. Tails wagging, the Alsatians trot into the courtyard and sniff a scent trail criss-crossing the rockery. "They were timid at first, but they're protective of their territory now. They'd do more than bark if anyone ran towards us." He bends low, viewing her from the dogs' perspective. His shirt is partly unbuttoned; the softness of cotton and the starkness of white in sharp contrast to his firm chest with silken black hairs, creeping into sight.

When she steps forwards her ankle buckles. Crying in alarm, she falls, hitting paving stones, grazing her knee on a corner of the rockery. A hand grips her shoulder. She twists to squint up to Cameron's face – a cream-coloured cloud.

He asks, "Have you fainted before?"

Shards of irritation shoot through her. "I didn't faint, I fell," she says indignantly, and cups her hands over the knee that had taken the brunt of the force.

"It will hurt," he says, "and then it will be better."

If only life could be as simple as that. She flexes her ankle. Unprepared practically and emotionally for this, she attempts to clamber to her feet.

Cameron's smile exudes humour and warmth. He talks gently, as though she is a child. "That was a very pretty dress." He pulls her up, links her arm in his. "You're going to be okay."

She wipes perspiration from her forehead. Tries to blink tears away.

"Come, you need a drink." He guides her to a side door.

After the brightness outside, the severe darkness indoors is blinding. She gropes for something solid. They pass through a laundry room and enter a spotless white-tiled open-plan kitchen. An archway leads to the hall. They continue through to the dining room, then a spacious living room with minimal furnishing and French windows opening out onto the courtyard.

Cameron's eyes slide over her. "I don't like fuss," he says.

She stops fussing with her hair.

"The trees running behind this house were taller and thicker than in the front gardens, and it was quite private," he says unexpectedly. "I shouldn't have had them cut down."

She sinks into a leather settee, the shade and texture of aubergine skin. Afternoon sunshine strays through the windows, making polished wooden surfaces gleam, shining a spotlight on her face, her throbbing head. But the effort to get up from the settee is too much. Her hands twist idiotically in her lap.

He undoes two more buttons on his shirt, loosens the belt of his trousers, closes the blinds to shut out the sun. A keen blade of light shears stubbornly through a slit between the slats.

She hunches up, clasping her arms around her body. There is silence. A faint aroma of sandalwood. She doesn't know what to do or say. Her sprained ankle pulsates. Discomfort swells into an insane panic.

He wraps a cold dampened cloth around her ankle. "Hold that until it burns." He selects a bottle from the wine rack. He clamps the bottle between his knees, twists a corkscrew in. His jaw muscles ripple. Everything about him is immaculate and ordered. His well-toned physique defined by the bright white shirt. The strong features in profile. His aquiline nose. Yet there is a boyishness to his demeanour, and he looks softened somehow.

"You gave Rachel my address?" Koliwe asks.

"Obviously."

She searches his face with a warning frown.

"Let's talk about this later." He settles beside her, then siphons wine into his mouth through outstretched lips. "Have I told you about my first job with an NGO?" He recalls being fresh to development work, the long hours, arduous conditions, pressed with urgency throughout. Back then he was based in Khartoum, Sudan – that was where his wrestle with the mechanics of aid truly began. "Expenses were generous. Bills were never paid with our salaries. There was no need. We had regular overseas holidays. Sudanese cultural values differ from ours." Formal education, he explains, was virtually non-existent. Education for all wasn't a maxim. Elderly men were cultural cornerstones.

Elders passed traditions on; without them, social structures collapsed.

"But Western aid prioritises children," Koliwe says.

"And U.K Aid thrust western ideologies upon them. You'll remember, we were exhorted to donate, while images of starving children popped up on our TV screens. The Sudanese, people famed across Africa for their gentility and hospitality, were presented by the west as helpless. Savages." He splashes more wine into Koliwe's glass.

The wine's musky scent, scarlet, seductive, erases the distress on her face. Her awkwardness evaporates. "What's the future of aid?" she asks, as she dissolves.

"Understanding problems at grass roots level. Promoting cultural knowledge exchange. The British media fuels the hysteria. We must shift from emergency programmes to sustainable long-term development. Employ female agriculturalists, as you outlined in your speech. U.K Aid must build upon our history of helping girls running child-headed families."

"Give aid without strings attached."

"True. Monies are diverted to causes that benefit the donor countries' interests. For every dollar Sudan received from U.K Aid, they now owe the World Bank ten." He straightens out his legs and stretches his body as luxuriously as a cat. Then he rises and plants himself on the plush Oriental rug before the French windows. "You've settled in well. You've got a great future." The pitch of his voice falls to a pastoral tone. "You're too vulnerable alone in town in that flat. You can't speak siSwati. You'll need security." Swinging round to face her, he says sharply and insistently, "Stay at my house while I'm away." He paces the rug with dramatic intensity – a well-rehearsed actor warming up for performances. "It's a protective community. There's plenty of privacy. You'll be safe. Swaziland – Mbabane in particular – is a strange place." The glass mirrors his approach as, gazing over the courtyard, he steps closer to the French windows.

The wine has gone to her head, but strength returns to her voice now his back is turned. "We hardly know each other."

"The only way to get to know me is to take some sort of risk." He walks behind her.

When she swivels round to face him, his eyes glisten like fool's gold.

"You know I'm attracted to you." Breezily, he moves on. "Come, I'll show you the rest of the house."

He takes a passage from the living room. She follows like an injured bird flying to the hunter. Finally, they enter a master bedroom with a dressing room and end-suite bathroom. The walls are pale gold. Sumptuous, velvety, saffron-yellow curtains fall to the deep pile carpet; a flounced duvet overhangs a king-size bed.

"I sleep in this room," he says, to continue the tour mood.

Another tide of envy sweeps across her as she thinks of her dreary bedsit. "I like how it's so... uncluttered. You have all this to yourself?"

"Yes." He is staring beyond the courtyard to his elegant gardens. "This house has its own servants' quarters." He draws the curtains right back. "Two rooms. It's adequate. Better than they'd have at the homestead."

The main house is joined to another dwelling by the double garage to form three sides of the courtyard.

Cameron swivels round. "Suits me. It's empty when I'm travelling."

Nervously, she glances into the garage. The guard has gone. The dogs lie under their master's car, spread flat in partial darkness on the cool concrete floor.

She sits cautiously on the edge of the bed, reflected in the mirror inlaid in the wardrobe's melamine doors. Cameron follows her gaze. He focuses on her wide mouth, sculptured cheekbones. There is Xolile. Her complexion has darkened during the past month to the richness of browned caramel. Her hair is a frizzy untamed wilderness. Her eyes bore into the bedcover, then flicker icily up to his.

He seats himself beside her. "Exhausted," he sighs, and unties his shoes. "You're shivering," he murmurs. "What's the matter?"

"Nothing."

"Sure? No one can see us." Again, he addresses her as though she is a child. "No one comes in here, except me." He flops onto the duvet's softness.

She cannot take her eyes from his body. Heat floods into her face. There is a desire to touch his skin. To lie down with him. And she allows the tingling sensation to spread from between her legs, to take over her body. Bringing her closer and closer to him, he licks and nibbles at her ear.

"We've got the house to ourselves." He kisses her face gently as if she is his, and, for this instant, the most important thing to him in the world.

"I can't. Please, not now," she whispers. She is trying to find a way to explain her inconsistencies, which so often make her mute, while the threat of HIV hangs above their heads like a noose.

Xolile murmurs, *Leave now. Before it's too late.* Fast as a ferret, she tears from the bedroom, grabs her keys, runs through the house to the courtyard and her car. Her heart gallops, a slim swish of cornflower-blue flies to the bedsit. Climbs the darkened staircase.

The building is quiet. Her unknown but felt part lies down. Her hair on the pillow is damp against her cheek.

CHAPTER ELEVEN

The next morning her ankle is bruised blue. She has difficulty getting out of bed. She wriggles about, listening to the radio news before kicking off the covers.

Cameron is already busy when she arrives at work. Preoccupied with papers, he speaks without looking up, "Your food report, Koliwe, when will that be ready?" His voice is demanding, yet demure. The red cotton scarf is tied rakishly about his neck. He rolls his shirt sleeves and, seeing her hesitation, smirks. His movements are loose, his seasoned complexion high-coloured, as though from a Romany life. He runs his fingers through greyish-brown curls, then reaches beneath his desk to close his briefcase.

She is caught in a tangle of emotions she does not understand.

She flicks through a file. Notices his lips. There is a pang of regret. Xolile ghosts across her skin. She hates him. Can't forget what happened at his bungalow – the cause, not the cure of pain. She should report him, though an accusation of harassment would be like unpinning a hand grenade.

By midday, the office is almost empty. Phepile has disappeared on a five-day field trip.

"Coffee?" Cameron is thick-necked from behind, and when he returns with two steaming cups, his expression is benign. "Let's discuss the irrigation programme," he says to Koliwe.

"I'd planned my research for late December."

"Late December? You won't find many people available to you in the field, most Swazis are involved with traditional duties," he says hurriedly, and pauses. "Something's the matter. We ought to talk."

Her heart floods with relief.

"I care about you, Xolile. I feel bad about yesterday." He takes something from his trouser pocket, while continuing to admonish himself, "I'm sorry. It won't happen again. Here, a gift. From the market." The small mahogany casket he plants on her palm has been elaborately carved.

Holding the ornament up to the light, she picks out the intricate ivory inlay. "It's adorable."

When she smiles, sensibility and tenderness stir in her eyes.

He rests his hip against her desk. "You don't know much about Swazi culture."

"Not much," she replies.

"Do you know *anything*?"

A guilty presence lurks in the air. She is aware of dampness under her arms. She is a misfit, a fake. "No. Well," she says evasively, "maybe, a little, yes."

"Soon there's Incwala," he says with the Xhosa click.

She repeats, "Incwala?"

He inclines his head slightly. "Sure."

She knows something about this. "It's an annual celebration. There's a ritual... for boys?"

"Yes, the old year is cast out in place of the new. It's around Christmas time."

"But what happens?"

"Young boys from all over Swaziland march together to fetch Lusekwane branches. They arrive at Lobamba at sunset and use the branches to build a corral, called a sibaya, a holding pen for cattle."

"It's a virility ceremony. A test of purity and strength?"

"The boys must all be virgins, and hundreds of warriors dance all day. There's a lot of dust flying about as they work themselves into a frenzy. The boys throw a black bull to the ground and the bull is beaten to death by the boys' bare hands. Though nowadays they use a special spear. Naked, the king straddles the bull, then..." chuckling, he performs a pelvic thrust. "But you won't be allowed to watch that bit." He is retying the neck scarf. The cloth is dyed a dull, ochre-red colour. It is the pigment of the African earth, red earth, almost the colour of bull's blood.

"I'll take you to Incwala."

*

On Saturday, the wind howls, swirling around street corners, bending brittle branches of crooked trees, buffeting buildings' high-pitched roofs. She passes under the tossing mauve of jacaranda in heavy bloom. Cuts between rows of ramshackle stalls in the covered market. Spinach sprawls from pannier baskets; charcoals smoulder beneath charred sweet corn. Tendrils of smoke swoon around a gaggle of girls, knots of haggling women. She has a peculiar feeling, passing a traditional healer's hut; snakeskins, small animal skulls, bags of white powder strung on twine tied to nails, sway in the doorway. Silver lightning slashes the sky; an acrid smell of burning wood floods the air. The way light falls, and the way women, shrouded in a sulphur-coloured vapour, cross busy roads with baskets, buckets, bundles of clothes upon their heads, is no longer new. Some wear berets, others have their hair oiled and plaited in tight cornrows. Others, their hair styled high and round in the traditional sicolo style. The market women squawk and caw at her in siSwati. The men, who are whistling and staring, must think she is from Mozambique, for they shout the few Portuguese words they know. No matter where she is in town, mountains are visible. Slabs of rock glisten where water weeps like blood from a graze, reminding her of her father's oil paints leaking from tubes to a jumble of overalls fallen from pegs, coats, cloths, shoes. Preoccupied with her father's paintings, which seem somehow to be lodged within her, she leaves the market, wades through the wailing wind to the end of Allistair Miller Street. Crowds flow, river-like, and divide. Her thoughts meander to her mother. She leans against a low stone wall, where men huddle together smoking cigarettes; the wraps of material clothing their loins flutter in the squall. A young girl pushes her into a kiosk. Another girl, trying to sell plastic bags, shoves forwards. Thandi's face was shaped like hers. Another, tarted up in a floral frock and a red wig, offers to sing a song. Koliwe hates the cold wind. Cruel sun. These stupid people. Their beastly illness. She scuttles along an alley, stumbling over broken bricks, pushes through the tide of men swaggering in smart suits, or stealing by in rags for clothes; their eyes, like the light, are sulphurous. Slips between women wearing a gay array of patterns, colours. Blends into the background. Four fountains at the top end of town pump majestically from the middle of the roundabout; the sloshing water audible through the steady drone of traffic.

Cameron's Land Rover drives past, circles the roundabout, pulls over and stops. He wears an old flannel shirt, the chequered print a faded blue, the top two buttons open; around his throat, the scarf of crimson cotton. Poking his head from the window, he bellows, "I'm driving across the border to South Africa, Ermelo. What're you doing today?"

She reels off a list of chores, finishing quietly with, "I'm changing money at the bank."

"The local currency, Emalangeni, can only be used in this country, it isn't accepted anywhere else."

"Yes, thank you, I know, I've been here two and a half months."

"Hop in," he says. "Don't bother with the bank, I'll lend you a few hundred rand."

She should make an excuse. Tell him she is not interested. He caresses the stubble under his chin, then pulls at an earlobe. Xolile battles within. Seemingly oblivious to the internal havoc he wreaks, he talks about Malalotja Nature Reserve where he once worked as a warden.

"Can we go to the reserve one weekend?" she asks.

"Sorry, I can't entertain you. I have a ward. Gift. She's from the countryside. I spend as much time with her as I can."

Here is a man who takes his work home. Koliwe leans forwards, impressed and intrigued; hair swirls around her nose and glues to her forehead.

"Gift's at boarding school." He adds, "In Nelspruit."

"Gift stays with you at weekends?"

"No, I visit her. Sobukwe, my driver, dropped her yesterday. She'll stay till the end of term." He shakes his head slowly. "Girls who go home at weekends get poor course marks."

Such detail is unexpected. The weight on her feet shifts, she feels the scales tip. "How old is Gift? Does she have brothers, sisters?"

"About ten," he says noncommittally. "Hei, are you gonna stay at my place while I'm away?" His eyebrows crinkle. His teeth clasp his bottom lip. "Pack some stuff tonight, you won't need much. Come over tomorrow."

Koliwe weighs up the pros and cons. The wind gusts have mellowed. A breeze pats her cheeks gently as a powder puff. She finally accepts his invitation with a coquettish grin.

She folds clothes carefully. Never had she imagined living in this dismal hovel.

Only now, as she digs between settee cushions, does she discover another of Rachel's cigarettes. She sets up the easel, wets the paper, lets it shrink back. The half-finished portrait, sketched with pen and ink, has a dark skin tone with a sepia tint; delicate shading under the chin. The determined expression and depth of emotion, the stark stare of his eyes, captured by wax charcoal pencils, mirrors the conflict within her. She tilts the dressing table looking glass by its wooden frame. There is a phantom of herself. Her eyes are her father's. Worry. Isolation swirls in the blue haze, the frustration-filled room where the smoke, the mirrors, the haunted reflections, the merits and morals of aid. Of giving. Gifts. The concrete walls, the ceiling, create a madness around and within. If she falls to the floor, will she shatter?

Lugging the suitcase from the doorway, she takes one last look at the dingy kitchenette, through the arch to the bedsitting room. Sunlight through bars.

PART TWO

CHAPTER ONE

She swerves from the driveway onto the Tea Road. The heat has not yet intensified, and expectation fills the air. The two Alsatians bound up to meet her at the gates, followed by Cameron; red chequered shirt tucked into his jeans, eyes contemplative. When she steps from her car, the line of staff in the courtyard waiting to see what she looks like, hurries indoors.

Cameron's fingers slide habitually through the grey-brown curls. He says, "This morning you look beautiful," a grin spreading across his face.

"Thank you," she replies, "for letting me stay."

"Ja, my pleasure." He leans towards her. The stubble on his chin buffets her cheek; his lips pucker into a kiss. He tells the guard to take her luggage, then strides into the kitchen, where a maid is washing up. He introduces Rose in a steady, low voice.

Rose's blue rubber gloves squeak against anything they come in contact with, setting Koliwe's teeth on edge. Suds drip from her gloves to the tiled floor.

Another maid dries dishes and chatters to Rose in siSwati. The maids wear black pinafore dresses, crisp, chalk-white aprons; frilly bonnets perch upon their heads.

"Queenie is the housekeeper," Cameron tells Koliwe.

Queenie smiles in reply. She has a fine, firm face. Intriguing, prominent, violet-brown lips and the bump of heavy pregnancy.

"Nice to meet you," Koliwe says.

"Queenie, say hello," Cameron orders.

"Hello, Miss Xolile. We're..."

Cameron breaks in, "Queenie's English isn't good."

Rose stacks crockery inside cupboards; with her shining eyes, light build, smart attire, stick-thin legs, she resembles a sparrow hopping about the room.

Sunlight streams through the open door to the bright airy kitchen, spangled with the dusty-gold specks drifting in from the gravel roads. The soft-hued rays are transparent, yet appear as solid as railway sleepers. Here, it is easier to breathe. Already Koliwe feels lighter.

Cameron crosses to the sink, swings round to face the door, excluding the maid from the conversation. "Rose will help if you need anything."

Rose wriggles her hips, straightens the pinafore skirt and frilly white apron, then carries the laundry basket into the back garden.

Snarling, their sharp white fangs on show, Cameron's dogs skulk around the doorway. He mutters, "Get out, you brutes." His sudden harshness is difficult to interpret.

Queenie shelters her bulge protectively and selects newly laid eggs from a basket on the sideboard to fill a shelf slotted into the fridge door. Like the flowers in the garden, Queenie's skin is flushed in the morning light with a precious glow.

The dogs slink around their master, sniffing, whining, wagging tails.

"Out of the kitchen! Get out!" he bellows.

His dogs obediently scuttle.

From the doorway is a view beyond the gardener's cottage to the main gates. A man potters in a plot with six scarlet flame trees at the far end of a lawn. Children, all girls, run about him in bursts of colour and energy.

"Nathi!" Cameron hollers. "Nathi, come here!" He checks his watch. "Nathi is the gardener. He's Queenie's husband. Their baby's due in about six weeks." He wheels round, affords Koliwe a heart-warming smile. "The guard is unloading your cases. Give your keys to him, I'll make sure he parks your car beside mine in the garage."

Rose's singing resonates around the back garden as she hangs shirts scrubbed blue-white on the washing line, pegs clamped between her teeth. Each bold decisive action possesses the spirit of a woman who stands up to bullies.

"Rose had a husband," Cameron says quietly to Koliwe. "Well," he corrects himself, "a man. He worked in South African mines, returning to Mbabane a few times a year."

Despite the pristine white wall tiles, the spotless floor, Koliwe is aware of imperfections. Between Cameron's lines are stories of miners sleeping twenty to a room. Of other wives desperate for money, becoming sex workers.

He strides through the house expecting her to follow. His brusque manner borders on dismissiveness. "I'm rushing," he explains. "In an hour, my plane leaves for Mozambique."

She wants to ask how long he will be gone, but he has disappeared to pack. She knows what her mother would have thought. She looks at the mountains, which are bold and noble, and feels small, inadequate, and trapped.

Lopsided with the weight of luggage, Cameron tramps past her through the hall and open-plan kitchen. He tells the guard to get his car. His red-checked shirt flaps against his back; his leather shoes crunch loudly on the gravel driveway. He loads his attaché case and computer and drives away having barely said goodbye.

That evening, when Koliwe returns to the bungalow, Queenie says a woman rang for Mr Cameron. Two days later, the woman calls again.

Koliwe enjoys the first week Cameron is in Mozambique. As soon as she returns from work, she runs to the end of the garden to knock on the squat little cottage door. Clay pots and tin pans are stacked on the verandah. Cane stalks crunch underfoot. A girl wearing a strip of cloth for a skirt sits crossed-legged in the dirt beside two grinding stones for grain. She looks up, grinning, when Koliwe slips through the doorway. A scent of rain-damp earth and maize blackened over a fire rises from the beaten dung floor. Rain has washed away the red mud packed around stones in the wattle frame, leaving chinks in the walls for the wind to wail through. In the dilapidated kitchen, with its corrugated zinc roof, chunks of mud have collapsed from corners coarse and crumbly as sand. Nathi and Queenie's daughters eat pumpkin, corn, millet, beans, while the afternoon sun glows through the west-facing windows. A threadbare curtain dangles for a door to the room where they sleep. Sometimes Koliwe folds her sleeves back to her elbows, captures her ocean of hair with an ivory clasp and helps Queenie prepare slaai – dicing avocados, crushing peanuts, squeezing lemons.

Nathi slaps her back amicably. "How are you, Sisi?"

Koliwe asks questions. How long will Cameron be gone?

Stooped over the kerosene cooker, weary with pregnancy, Queenie twists to Koliwe with a pained smile. "He said his research would keep him away three weeks."

Koliwe squints at the mackerel sky; clouds trail like a marbled curtain through which sunlight splays. She is remembering how he reacted to the lightning at the Johnstons' drinks party. How his turbulent interior is masked by a thin veneer of calm. Why has she trusted him? But she has not, completely. He swings like a pendulum between promise and poison.

Queenie confirms what Koliwe knows, but would prefer to pretend she does not. "You better watch out, girl."

Koliwe suppresses the hollow sensation of dread. Eyes the maid suspiciously.

Queenie adds, "People don't look when they don't want to see."

"Why tell me to be careful with Cameron?"

Queenie doesn't answer immediately. Her copper eyes turn down.

Supicious, Koliwe presses further. "Who keeps calling him?"

Queenie straightens in her quiet, dignified manner.

Nathi has placed a hotly burning kerosene lamp on a metal stand. The flame distorts his features. "Before the sun sets, Xolile, you must join us for something to eat." He averts his eyes when addressing her. "Electricity doesn't come this far," he grunts.

The air bears a beefy aroma from a gurgling, whining stew. The girl comes in from grinding grain to smooth the crumpled tablecloth. The lamp exhales smoky black plumes and casts strange shapes on the mud walls.

At first light, Queenie's daughters set up stalls for the early Thursday morning markets. Sometimes they sleep on the roadside, then carry on their heads baskets of home-grown sesame, or bundles of wattle heavy enough for two or three men. The girls share the same bed, oil and plait each other's hair, bake scones to sell together, drink sugary, red hibiscus tea, weave grasses into rope – their sweat mingling with a sweeter scent of acacia blossoms. Koliwe sneaks gifts for them from Mbabane – soaps, vials of perfume.

Whether she is sitting in the bungalow, on the red Persian carpet gazing through the French windows onto the gardens and the long low evening sun, or at the office, in a daze, reading stacks of reports on methods of improving food production, writing faxes, booking flights, typing memos, day in, day out, she thinks of him. Of a shared intimacy. Then is grasped by a fierce shame. Because of the gap at the heart of herself. Because she isn't here to obsess over a man, her boss, especially.

The move from the bedsit coincides with a new phase in her work. Her days are spent in the field researching the vulnerability of rural communities. For the last three years, Swaziland's rainfall has been low. She focuses on U.K Aid's irrigation programme set up by the Mbabane Small Farm Development Project. The project gives grants to Swazi farmers to start model plantations of their own. On one fifth of their land, the farmers can grow what they like, but sugar has to be grown on the other four fifths. She drives to a major plantation to survey the ratoons. Most of the crop has been harvested. Huge bundles of seed cane are stacked. Row upon row of stubble spreads, women wield shovels, turning mud for the water to flow through the heavy reddish soil, visible at the end of each row; a few workers stoop, tending new shoots.

Katerina, Sambulo and Hlengiwe often gather beside the photocopier in the back-office. They disperse when Koliwe walks in. She senses secrets are whispered about her. Phepile goes about her business confidently, dressed in a pink blouse, blue slacks, open-toed sandals.

Catching up on paperwork, Koliwe gives Phepile her quick smile. "Why does Cameron disappear for such a long time?"

"He's developing funding proposals. And says he's been helping that child, Gift."

"I'm living at his house while he's away." Koliwe wipes dust from the desk with the flat of her hand, then leans against the filing cabinet. "He tried to kiss me."

"I hope you fought him off." Phepile gives the sharpest of looks. "You didn't? Is that the sort of man you want?"

Koliwe hangs her head. "I know some men are after one thing."

"Yes, some men can charm birds from the trees." Phepile shakes her head, laughing. The air about her is light, untroubled.

Koliwe hitches down her top, which had ridden up at the waist. "Do you think I should check on Thandi?" she asks. "Try to find that shack?"

"I've been. The place was empty." Phepile's face becomes taut, her lips a tight line.

Watching, Koliwe adjusts the neckline of her chiffon blouse. How unlike the women at the Johnstons' party Phepile is, with their quick, insolent glances and trivial utterances, their eyes poked into puffy white faces caked in make-up, like currants lost in dough.

CHAPTER TWO

In her purse is the chit of paper Maureen had given her. She dials Maureen's number. They arrange to meet for lunch the next day at Mandela's Restaurant.

In the morning, she roots through the wardrobe, pulls out a silky gold dress dotted with tawny flowers. She fumbles with the zip and the material rips. She takes a shower; struggles into a sage-coloured wrap-over robe.

An oily rainbow of shades shimmers on the tarmac road. Gaily dressed women stroll beneath the blossoming trees; colourful birds sing in the branches. The sky is a windless blue canopy. The market, a jamboree of colour. A yellow and mauve striped awning shades the doorway to Mandela's Restaurant. The décor is elegant, chairs with scroll feet, plush satin-covered upholstery.

Maureen is stationed towards the back, a smoking cigarette clamped between her lips. "Hello darling," she announces.

A skinny waiter draws a chair back for Koliwe, lights the candles on their table, then waddles through scarlet pools of light.

"I hope you're not going to talk politics," Maureen says. She orders a carafe of Pinot Noir. Despite living under a scorching sun, her skin is as pallid as tracing paper, her eyebrows so blonde they barely show. The dull red from the lights glances across shiny waves of her yellow hair; her eyes glimmer blue. She has the classic looks of a 1920s American film star. The waiter pours chilled wine. Maureen's tone mellows. Solemnly, she sips the wine; her cheek bones sharply defined in decreasing light.

"Just been fluttering around, have you darling?" Maureen emits a hollow chuckle. "What will you have to eat?" her voice creaks. She hails the waiter and says grandiosely, "Une bouteille de Merlot, s'il vous plait."

Hedging around tables with an impoverished look, the waiter returns. Maureen swishes the damson-coloured liquid in the bottom of her glass. The waiter hovers behind their chairs, retreating once their order has been taken.

Koliwe sighs, shaking her head. "I'm not sure about my job."

"Why did you come to Mbabane in the first place?"

Why do you run? And from whom? From feelings of incompleteness? Ghosts of the past? Koliwe says, "I needed a change." A yearning for home ripples through her body. She thinks of Scotland. Her father's paintings of Inverness. She is with him by the sea; the beach desolate; windswept. Sand covered in snow. Before her mother died, life seemed immaculate and ordered. She hopes she can find a new self. Won't slip into old routines. Wedged between different kinds of oppression.

The food arrives quickly, spicy meatballs with a cucumber dip and some things resembling raw chipolatas, which Koliwe does not manage to eat.

"I'm not at Pine View," Koliwe says. "I'm staying at Cameron's."

Maureen's look is calculating. She lights another cigarette.

"Maureen, you know Cameron well. Can I ask something? He says he's helping a girl. Gift."

Maureen pauses and looks away. Then begins, "It's not the first time he's 'helped' a girl." Her fingers draw inverted commas in the air. "Took the first one under his wing. Paid her school fees. She's quite a success. Can't remember her name…" Raising her eyebrows, Maureen looks in earnest at the ceiling, as if the name could be written up there. "They were…" she hesitates, "close. Anyway, that was years ago."

Maureen's sight flicks to Koliwe's brown eyes, gentle expression. Unable to meet Maureen's look, Koliwe pushes food around her plate.

Maureen twirls a ringlet around one finger. Like a river, she is constantly changing. "All women are mad," she branches off suddenly. "We drink too much. Smoke too much. Live off pills."

The bony waiter creeps behind Maureen's chair with another bottle of wine. His voice is softer than dark brown sugar. Maureen stifles a burp. One of the candles has flickered to nothing.

The women head for the market where men sell potatoes and oranges in stacks, or apples in plastic bags hanging from the ceilings of their shacks. With arms linked, they thread through the afternoon crowds as though their lives have been interwoven for years.

The news that Queenie has given birth reaches Cameron's bungalow at nightfall. As word spreads, the little cottage at the end of the garden fills with family members congratulating Nathi on the birth of his first son.

Koliwe unearths her spectacles from the clutter on the table. She peers through the French windows. In the pale light, clouds are visible. Nathi stands in the open doorway to his house. She slips outside and beyond the iron gates to congratulate him.

The dark garden blossoms with untold mystery, the air is thinly scented with jasmine and cedar wood. The moon has risen above lurid trees and peeps from behind the clouds when Nathi's shadowy figure strolls across the grass to the pond.

Koliwe is happy and concerned at once. "I am so glad you have a son – only the baby's early, isn't it?"

"Yes, he's early." Moonlight shines silver-blue upon Nathi's sable skin. "My wife gave birth at her family homestead. Truly, it is wonderful."

"Will you visit them?"

"I'll go to the top of the hill near Nhalangano, but I'll not go down to the hut."

"Why?" She watches the man's face.

The light is too dark to see his expression, but his agitated shrug indicates she should know the answer. "The father's not allowed till three months after the birth," he says. "On the fourth full moon I'll see my son. Before that, I cannot enter."

The stars are far apart; tiny sparkling lights in an expansive darkness. Koliwe looks to the brightest. It seems they are there for a purpose. This is the beginning of new things. The boy-child is a ray of hope bringing new life to the world.

Nathi seems restless. The pitch of his voice drops, "Many stars and one round moon," he murmurs as if lost, momentarily, in dreams swirling in the moonlit air. Then he says in his soft manner, "Will you and Mr Cameron marry... have children?"

Her heart skips a beat. A husband equals children. Children equal family. Family equals loss.

"Thank you, Xolile," he says, "for being here tonight."

"I'm glad for you." Moving to go, she adds, "I'd like to see your wife and child."

"Good. Tomorrow." Nathi gives a proud silent nod by way of another thank you.

She heads towards the well-lit interior of Cameron's bungalow, glimpsing Nathi over her shoulder before the dark shape that defines him disappears behind the gates.

The kitchen door bolts rattle.

"Hey! Mr Cameron!" Rose is shouting. *"Mr Cameron!"*

Koliwe strips the sheets back and leaps out of bed. The kitchen blinds are closed; morning sunlight seeps beneath the door.

Rose hollers defiantly, "Mr Cameron, come quickly! The baby's sick."

"Mr Cameron isn't here, Rose," Koliwe calls. She draws the bolts back. "Should I phone for a doctor?"

"No." Rose shakes her head. "You can drive the car. You *will* help, Xolile?" she cries desperately. "You'll bring Queenie's baby back?"

118

Koliwe must help somehow. She almost flies in her hurry to get out of the house. The sun, an orange strand, slices an indigo sky. The barking dogs rouse the new guard as she shoves open the garage doors.

Rose drags Nathi from the gardener's block. His eyes are swollen, his body shakes with sleep. They bundle him into the car, then tear along the gravel track and into a cool clear morning. Women carry grass for thatching, crops have started to grow. They pass schoolgirls in stark white blouses and brown pinafore dresses, a patchwork of small arable plots, then speed over the hill as sunlight races through the grasses, turning off at the dirt track to the homestead near Nhlangango.

Chickens scratch in the dust around the rondavel of plaited grass. Koliwe positions herself behind Rose in the open doorway. Queenie lies inside on a threadbare blanket draped across the metal bedsprings, her reddened face rigid with fatigue. She levers herself onto her elbows to sit upright. The place reeks of the unfamiliar – new life, stale sweat, fresh blood. Queenie puts the baby to her breast and tries to nurse him. Tears streak her cheeks and slide down to the little boy. Nathi's sister, Sophie, crouches beside Queenie's knees to support the baby's spine with her hands. A girl aged about four sits beside the bed, obstinately absorbed in pounding a postage stamp down with her fist, trying to make it stick on the earthen floor.

Rose whispers in Koliwe's ear, "Both grandmothers were at the birth." She points to a woman beside Queenie whose face is toughened by life. "That's Sabisile."

Sabisile ushers Koliwe further into the hut. Rose glances at Koliwe over her shoulder in doubtful expectancy, as if to say *Bring the baby back to life*. Koliwe realises the family sees her upbringing in the west as a source of special powers.

Sabisile disentangles the baby from his mother's arms and snuggles him against her own cheek. His puffy eyelids are welded together. Koliwe shakes her head when Sabisile holds the baby out to her.

"Take him," Sabisile says.

But breath no longer moves in the infant's chest. Koliwe is completely powerless, and feels increasingly feeble as the strength of the sun burns her back. Her mother is dying of cancer, propped up with pillows in bed. There is no body movement; her face is whiter than the sheets. Koliwe climbs the ladder of anxiety. She wants, needs, to succeed at this. She is burdened with guilt and responsibility, as if she herself creates death. Xolile stirs. Aware of her own weight and shape, of the pressure of the baby's fragile head in the fold of her arm.

"Thank you, Xolile." Sabisile relieves her of the boy-child's body, then returns him to her daughter's arms.

Three women make their way across a stony hillside towards the birth hut, carrying water from the river by balancing tin buckets on their heads. The first bears a lemon-yellow coverlet; the second, a woven necklace of rushes; the third, bundles of baby clothes.

Leaning from the window, Sabisile waves. "Your sisters have come," Sabisile says to Queenie, walking to the doorway to greet them.

Nathi is motionless, as though he has been dreaming, and at the sound of Sabisile's voice, awakes. Anguish shows in his dark brown eyes, agony in the lines of his brow.

Sabisile avoids his gaze, muttering, "Say it isn't true."

Queenie's sisters lift the buckets from their heads to place them by the door. Three shimmering circles of water calm; the sheen on the surfaces, gleaming like sovereigns, reflects the yellowish dawn.

The first sister does not enter. The second kisses the baby's forehead, then runs from the hut. The last drops the coverlet in the doorway, falls to her knees on the reed mat and covers her face with both hands.

Queenie sings softly to the tiny limp form clasped to her breast. The baby's head lolls to one side under her chin. Nathi pushes past Koliwe and peels his son's body from Queenie's dress. Nathi's wife becomes silent. Nathi carries the baby in the crook of one arm, cradled to his chest. The little head rests in the palm of his hand.

Rose passes Nathi the folded coverlet. He opens it, spreads it over the body. Two skinny legs poke from beneath. Nathi touches tiny crinkled hands, still warm, supple. He moves the delicate fingers. Ten tiny toes.

"They work well," he says.

Queenie lies on the coarse blanket and shields her tear-stained face. Sabisile puts her arms about her daughter. Nathi's cheek muscles flex and contort; wrinkles flow across his brow; the corners of his mouth twitch as he swallows. His eyes are laden with unshed tears.

Koliwe is the intruder at a family gathering. And yet Nathi takes her hand and holds it in his, close to his son's lifeless body.

"I'm the father," Nathi says to her. "See," he adds, grimacing. "They look like my hands. Mamma's face too." Lifting the baby to give to his sister, Nathi turns heavily and takes leaden strides from the rondavel and out across the hills.

Sabisile and Sophie carry the baby on a tiny wooden bier and carefully position the body in the posture of the newly born, and the dead. Elbows close to his sides, forearms upwards.

The return journey is slow. The sun's rays stream across pineapple fields, striking the slender tips of leaves and defining their sharpness. Rose says this is the fifth baby Queenie has lost. Although the mourners do not cry out loud, their inconsolable grief, a wail of agony, is sustained in the blue air.

CHAPTER THREE

Cameron rests his chin on steepled fingers. "You're surprised I'm here?" His eyes track her movements. "I returned from Botswana last week, but I've been staying at the Mountain Hotel," he adds by way of explanation. "U.K Aid has a suite there. Don't worry, I'll be home to see you tonight."

She scans his florid lips, the handsome bridge of his aquiline nose. Trying to understand the impatient weariness behind his greyish eyes. Eyes that can make her levitate or slide away with embarrassment. His sun-burned arms, silvering hair, bristled chin, the slight frown he often wears.

"How's your research?" he asks.

"I made a number of trips to the sugar plantations before and after harvesting." She explains how at first she got nowhere with local people. Upon arriving at a small-holding with her questionnaire, she was bombarded with requests for cigarettes, blankets, even cameras. Then she hired a translator, and once the farmers became used to her, concealed conflicts bubbled to the surface. The land the boreholes were on belonged to wealthy chiefs who charged small farmers exorbitantly. Farmers, unable to pay, borrowed from the chiefs at high interest rates. Local chiefs refused to drop interest or water rates, making many small farmers bankrupt. The situation was no better than it was before U.K Aid's boreholes were sunk.

"I'd hoped you'd find a solution." His tone is unsettling. He coughs to clear his throat. "I want you to compile the basis for a funding proposal for another irrigation programme," he concludes.

"There's little point in starting another until these conflicts are resolved," she says.

How he can slip from manager to friend back to manager, all while dictating a research brief? His face doesn't give any answers. Does he secretly dislike her? Has he suffered some terrible misfortune? Is he haunted by someone else? Do squalid thoughts run through his mind? Why does the breeze left in his wake blow with gusts of love and hate?

Trying to understand the impatient weariness behind his greyish eyes. Eyes that can make her levitate or slide away with embarrassment. His sun-burned arms, silvering hair, bristled chin, the slight frown he often wears. She scans his florid lips, the handsome bridge of his aquiline nose.

Tension simmers above the bungalow. Gun-metal clouds bulge and sag; a blanket of shadow is moored to the mountaintops. She sits listlessly in the Mazda. The heat is intense. A man she has not seen before weeds the rockery. His head ducks up and down amidst scarlet and pink irises. She swings the car door open. The Alsatians pad across the courtyard's granite slabs and nudge her with their heads.

Kneeling on the deep pile carpet, surrounded by electronical equipment – a laptop charger, extension leads, digital camera – she thumbs through her report on the squalor within a one-room home, where a mother starves herself to feed seven children.

The telephone rings. Lines crackle obstinately. She shakes the receiver.

Out floats a female voice, "Darling, It's me, Sindy."

"Who?" Koliwe asks.

The caller slams down the receiver.

The solid tread of Cameron's leather-soled shoes on the parquet hall floor makes Koliwe shiver.

"Who called?"

"Sindy."

His voice has an angry edge, "Sindy hung up?"

Koliwe nods. Her lips are pursed, her eyes screw. Two slits. "Where are Queenie and Nathi?"

"We have a replacement gardener."

The memory of holding Queenie's dying baby is too sharp. Determined not to let tears spill over her cheeks, again she asks, "Where are Queenie and Nathi?"

"Does it matter?" His nose wrinkles disapprovingly.

The atmosphere between them ferments. Has he seen the beads of perspiration on her forehead?

She twists from him, chews on her lower lip. "I spent a good deal of time with Queenie's family while you were away. Will you drive me to their baby's funeral?"

Unable to disguise his surprise upon hearing her raised voice, he fidgets impatiently with his shirt collar. "I *told* you about the birth. You should've rushed Queenie and her baby to Johannesburg Hospital. Instead, the thing died in your arms. Isn't that what you said?" His delivery is mechanical, and he looks nonplussed, as though he has never had to wrestle with pain and loss. "Mr Callow returns next week, he'll expect your progress report."

She can tell Cameron thinks she is trouble. The attack on the girl. The police inquiry. Queenie's baby dead.

From an opened cardboard box, he unpacks a figurine – a pregnant woman carved from ebony wood. His cheeks suck in. His eyebrows pull together. He turns the gleaming body in his hands, the look in his eyes is as primeval as hunger. He is retreating from feelings he once had.

"We're close one minute, then you go away," she says.

"That's what it's about," he replies sourly.

His woodenness, and the pleasure he appears to derive from fondling the carving, disgusts her.

He checks his watch. "I'm late." His face is steel; his eyes, pewter. "I don't believe you staying here is working."

Her heart erupts. By late afternoon, she is so angry she does not notice the sunlight glancing on the valley. The little children pass with hopeful, begging hands. Does not notice the sweet-smelling grass, cut that morning, has dried now, or the guard who rakes it in.

At sunset, the guard is nowhere to be seen. Cameron is furious. He begins setting the house alarms in preparation for the night. There is fire in his eyes and in his stride.

They set off in absolute darkness. It is nearly four a.m. The stars have faded; the headlights' pearly glow burrows into a sky thicker and blacker than treacle.

Koliwe sits beside Cameron in the front of his Land Rover, clutching a bunch of white lilies with a dense perfume. Rose directs from behind, seated beside Rachel. Koliwe, pleased to see her aunt again, glances back at them, then does a double take. In this country everyone knows everyone else.

Dawn is breaking by the time they near the part of the Malkerns Valley where Odai, Nathi's brother, lives. Rose taps Cameron's shoulder for him to slow down. They are on the edge of a rough township. The vehicle weaves between homesteads containing a mixture of houses — some built of concrete, others mud, sticks and grasses. Rachel explains there will have been a night vigil. Cameron sighs with relief when the headlights pick out the landmark Rose had described: a breeze-block house central to a run-down homestead.

He parks alongside a tarpaulin erected a short distance from the house. Women from outside the extended family sleep on the grass beneath.

"Queenie will have slept next to the coffin all night," Rachel says, drowsily.

"You should have worn black," Cameron mutters in Koliwe's ear. "I'll pick you up later."

Before leaving, he casts a momentary glance in Koliwe's direction; his irises changing hue like grey-green beads in a kaleidoscope. Deliberately she turns, slipping lightly from the Land Rover into the cool dark morning and the sea of confusion ahead.

One of the children runs to find Nonhlanhla, Queenie's sister-in-law, and Rachel, Rose and Koliwe are called into the bungalow. When they enter the room housing the baby's casket, the tiniest youngsters strike up a song. Koliwe wonders what to do with the flowers. No one else has any.

Candles fill a far table and a shelf to the left of the door; some have burned very low. About twenty women are seated on the floor. Nobody wears black; all the women wear headscarves and blankets around their shoulders. Sophie, Nathi's sister, emaciated, worn, moves slowly in a mauve cotton dress, a hazy bank of yellow behind her. A mass of tall thin flames lean away from the open doorway, quivering, responding to the slightest draught.

The shadowy figure of a young girl steps into the soft light. She introduces Koliwe to Nonhlanhla, speaking for her in siSwati, then joins Queenie and the other women by the glimmering candles. It is unclear whether the women are praying or paying their respects to the ancestors. After Koliwe's father became a Christian, he thought he was above traditional beliefs - but then Koliwe realises they are praying. She prays for Queenie and her family, for Rachel and Queenie's dead son.

Rachel points out Odai and his three children. The four men stand as though petrified before a rectangle of cloth pinned halfway up one wall, half-covering the casket. Odai draws the cloth aside. He undoes the pins to open the lid, then his frail form crumples against the wall. A cockerel crows in the yard outside. There is the swish of the concrete floor swept by the harsh bristles of a broom. These morning sounds slice through the quietness that contains the room.

Rachel pays her final respects. Koliwe follows in a slow, forlorn procession: their forms no more than shadows, their features subdued in the greyness of the dawn seeping from the window, through the candlelit room and onto the dead baby's face. The fragrance of pinewood rises from the white satin-cushioned casket. Shielding her eyes, Koliwe peers inside. The face holds the grace of those who sleep. The eyelids, not quite closed, reveal two brown-grey filmy slits. What is peculiar is the proximity the boy has to life. And the shocking sense of the irreversible.

There is spontaneous singing. Full and colourful waves of gospel rhythm wash through their bodies and, as the melody swells, Koliwe is literally moved, swaying to the refrain.

Everyone trails towards the door and mills around the homestead yard. She recognises Sipho from the florid scar on his cheek. The Zionists wear white, blue and red gowns. Inside was the smell of burnt wax and grass mats, outside is the summery aroma of hay and the brightness of the sun.

Rachel wanders to Koliwe and says, "Our second cousin, Senty, her baby died two weeks ago. Four months old." Rachel moves closer so as not to be overheard, "When it gets to funerals *every day...*" her voice trails off. They are living in a country full of ghosts.

The priest heads the procession to where about seventy newly dug mounds crowd an open hillside dotted with plastic flowers, stick crosses, mud-splattered tinsel and fluttering ribbons weathered by storms – all lit by the exhilarating morning light. Cobwebs glisten like small silver flags strewn across stems of grass. Koliwe links hands with the other women; many have walked here before. Their ancestors surround them, wading through grasses long and lush, wet with glistening spots where rainbows sparkle in the glass mirror balls rotating in each dew drop.

Odai bends forwards to scratch a cross shape onto a stone with a stick. The flimsy wooden casket is lowered between the grave's walls. Groups file past to throw red soil and stones upon the lid. Some sit amidst rush-like stems taller than the heads of those who stand, clinging to posies of jonquil-yellow lilies, tears shining on their cheeks. Sobbing, Sabisile pulls a bunch of plastic flowers from a black plastic bag and places her bouquet at the graveside. Then they all return to the homestead.

They wash the spirits of the dead from their hands in a pot by the doorway.

"Don't do that. It's a bit suspect," a man with a heavy crucifix hanging from his neck points out to Koliwe. He doesn't wear a Zionist gown; he must be a Christian. "Eighty percent of the population is involved in this witchcraft. Terrible, isn't it?"

Koliwe says, "I had no idea," and walks back to the grave. Like a wilted flower bent over the mound, she puts her bouquet on the dirt. Because her father would have wanted her to. Food is already prepared in the yard: roast chicken, rice, a savoury sauce, egg and potato salad, freshly slaughtered beef. Rachel tells Koliwe she and Rose will get a lift into town with Odai.

Mid-afternoon, Cameron returns. Small fires smoulder on the mountainsides and the pungent stench of cow dung wafts from cattle byres in the valleys. The air is terrifically hot, the sun burns her skin, hurts her eyes. She wishes she hadn't eaten the beef; the taste in her throat smells like cow dung.

The Land Rover reeks of Cameron's eau de cologne, a bitter mix of lemon and bergamot. He veers off the grass track onto gravel, the blue band of the Mdzimba Mountains lies in front.

"Good, was it?" he asks.

Flames of disgust blaze in Koliwe's veins. Her gaze strays across his Romanesque nose, hollow cheeks, jutting chin, stubborn expression. Layers of silence as thick and high as the mountains falls between them.

Cameron swerves onto the highway where Zionists amble, dressed in white. He brakes to avoid a cow sunning herself on the tarmac and, sticking his head from the window, yells, "What the hell's going on?"

Slothfully, the beast moves as a girl emerges from bushes leading a goat on a string, blocking the road again. Her hair is braided in zigzag patterns; her face murky-black like oiled paper.

Cameron leans towards Koliwe, briefly taking his eyes from the road. "You'd think they'd change their behaviour. Y'know what they say?"

"Tell me."

"Most of these girls are whores."

Although a dimple appears at the corner of his mouth, the curve of his lips soon straightens, and the flicker of a smile dissolves.

"How's Gift?" she asks.

"Fine." He winks at her as though they share a secret. "Xolile, aren't you the 'One Who Forgives'?"

An intense nausea wells in her throat. "Stop the car and let me out."

"What, here?" he says.

"Yes, I'm going to be sick."

He says, "Don't be silly," and laughs.

She leans over and slaps the side of his face. He must have seen her hand coming, yet didn't respond. The strike had the force of a tightly wound spring. She hadn't allowed herself time to be angry, and the nausea is gone.

Clouds form like ghosts' breath across a rose-coloured sky. His face turns a deep mango colour. He runs his palm across his chin. The slap has not given her gratification, although she can tell, from his watery eyes, his cheek burns from the rebuff.

He pulls up on the verge. "Look, I'm sorry," he says. "Let's make up. Will you, can you forgive?"

Koliwe/Xolile – a split soul. Two people within one body. Both think *No*. But Xolile hears Koliwe say, "Okay."

His eyes, grey-blue rock pools, hold her with their penetrating stare. She hasn't noticed until now the different shades: one slate-grey, the other a greyish-green. She recoils into the seat as the Land Rover rattles onto the road. Children stride like little knights defending the sandy verges. Strelitzia flash flamboyant orange flowers; their leaves glisten like latex and whisper in the wind, reminding her of trees she made at primary school with gauze and tenuous paper strips. Evening light filters into the vehicle. The windscreen, peppered with dust, is losing its transparency. Cameron drives vigilantly through monotonous scenery, trying to keep the tyres on tarmac, hurtling down a fast-disappearing road.

"About Gift," she finally says, "How come she's your ward?"

"It's simple. I'm a kind of uncle paying her school fees. She'll live in Mbabane after she's matriculated."

Children at the roadside wave, their hands pinkened by the evening sun, and a baby girl in a blue dress that keeps blowing open where buttons have undone. Sharp bends in the road take them lower and lower. Dim lights glow from within mud houses; villagers squat beside open evening fires. Goats move on slopes towards the bottom reaches, then all the lights sink from view, as the belt of road pushes through the cold blackness that engulfs the imposing mountain ranges on the descent to his lodge.

CHAPTER FOUR

Something collides with the windscreen with a thud. Cameron slams on the brakes. The Land Rover screeches to a halt.

"It's a widow bird. Used to catch them as a boy. Back then we called them jojo birds." He fumbles for a torch then melts into the darkness.

Cicadas chirrup in roadside bushes. Koliwe pushes on the interior light but can then see nothing of the scrub outside.

Cameron returns cradling something to his chest.

"Are you going to see if it can fly?" she asks, clambering from the seat.

"Wild animals kept in captivity for a time never survive when set free."

Moving towards her is the scent of the cooling savannah – an earthy aroma of animal dung, ammonia, night flowers' fragrances. Cameron's hands cage the trembling feathery body; making little jolting movements, its beak jabs through gaps between his fingers. She accepts the creature into her hands. The bird's glossy black head flops to one side in the L shape of her arm. She eases out a feather tip; the wing extends like a black fan. The eyes are tiny, bright, black beads until the crinkled pinky-brown eyelids close. Gently she sets the jojo bird down on taloned feet. It hops sideways, cocks its satin head; the beady eyes blink. Screeching, fluttering frantically in circles, the bird is able only to spread its one good wing. Queenie's baby flashes into Koliwe's mind as the slick black body launches – a dark lightning bolt full of revolt and rebellion shoots past her ear, then glides silk-smooth into a deep ravine.

Cameron gazes abstractedly into a shallow trough he has made in the gravel with his toe, as though searching for a meaning which can be found only by turning over stones.

"Why don't you like Maureen?" she asks, once they are on the road again.

"Look, Maureen's a mischief-maker," he replies briskly. "You've been talking to her?"

"I haven't seen her since the Mountain Hotel conference." When Koliwe lies, her body swells. Something – it feels like a lump of seaweed – rises in her throat.

The Land Rover rattles over a bumpy ridge and grinds to a halt. A vein of torchlight wavers before Cameron negotiating the stone path. He scopes the garden with the torch's beam and picks out a wattle and mud hut. The rondavel where Gift sleeps?

"Don't you get scared living alone in the mountains?" she asks.

"The place is protected by muti."

The torchlight illuminates a wooden carving of an aged squatting man about one metre away, partly concealed by wattle flowers and thorn trees; his head is distorted, strangely shaped.

"That's reassuring," she says.

"Locals believe in it. The Swazi are like children. Can't think things through as you and I do."

In discord, they mount the steps, their shadows slithering behind them. Was coming here a mistake? There is a click as he flips down a switch. A generator whirs; crude light floods the verandah. Cicadas chirrup a high-pitched melody then, seconds later, cease in unison as suddenly as they began. He pulls a bunch of keys from his pocket, fiddles one into the lock and rams the front door three times with his shoulder, before it is wrenched from its swollen frame.

The lodge looked deceptively small from the outside. The interior reveals many rooms leading from one another. The hopelessness that typifies the end of an era hangs about the hall, with its moth-eaten reedbuck heads dulled grey with dust; rows of stuffed birds staring glassily; a zebra hide stretches across floorboards which creak beneath the feet. Constructed of wood, the place retains the hunting lodge character. Ceiling to floor windows and timber walls with overlapping planks like the sides of a clinker-built dinghy. Blinds have been rolled down. A kerosene lamp with a tubular-shaped glass gleams like white gold on a cast iron stand, as if a maid or domestic help has prepared for Cameron's return.

He marches ahead to the living room.

She lifts a silver-framed photo from the metal chest: a stocky woman in a smock top and shorts with thickened arms and ankles, creamy-white skin, heavy cheekbones, denim-blue eyes. Black hair coils around her neck. The name Sylvia is inscribed in the frame's left corner. The camera has captured the woman's brave, confronting stare.

"Who's this?" Koliwe asks.

"Mother." Seizing the photograph, whispering, "Yup," Cameron gazes, unblinking, at the image. "Died in childbirth, after leaving me and Dad." He stares at the image stiffly, his eyes narrowing to slits. Koliwe can hear him thinking. He swears softly, pours a vodka, gulps it as if it were water, refills his glass. "Want a drink?" He pours another vodka, hands it to her.

She hesitates, then dares to let curiosity get the better of her. "Maureen's very knowledgeable about Swaziland country and…"

"Maureen grew up in a different country," he replies curtly. His jaw muscles move, indicating displeasure. "Yes, she came here at a time England was advertising for workers from the colonies. Now it's very different." He seems amused by what he said and gives a cynical grin. "Maureen brings her Scottish education here, calling it development. She's feeding the young a lie. Training them for jobs that aren't there. What can she teach in the rural areas? What's the use of formal education when there are no jobs?" he says abrasively. "With so many dying of AIDS, is it better to be educated, qualified for work, or illiterate and happy?" The humidity is high and the way he has tied the neck scarf seems to bother Cameron. With his grubby fingers he yanks at the knot, forcing it open, freeing the scarf from his throat. "Look at our influence. It's glaring you in the face what we've done." He shakes out the scarf in a slapdash manner, saying recklessly, "I don't believe we can help these people, Xolile."

"What do you mean?"

"There's a story about Hemingway" – he slaps at where a fly has settled on his face – "and some starving beggars he passed daily on the roadside. He wanted to help them so he gave them money, only to discover that, when he next went by, they had spent the money on a dog and were sharing their scraps with it. We have created so much dependency, if we help people read and write when literacy is not what they require, we detach them from their own kind, they become estranged, fitting into neither their own society, nor ours, because we don't make room for them, and the forests, their heritage, are gone. We might fence bits off, open national parks for our pleasure and make the local people pay to enter. We see their traditions as wasteful and, in the name of progress, think of all the money that could be made by them for us. But our ways are wasteful. Cars burn natural resources, washing machines, dishwashers, airplanes, the examples are endless. Our future is not sustainable. Theirs was."

"Education means choice." She rubs the back of her neck, the frown lines on her forehead are like deep cuts. "They need our help, surely?"

"We try to help, but who has really benefited? The money we get from the development projects pays for cars, houses, swimming pools, dinner parties. I don't think we've helped them at all." Koliwe starts protesting, but Cameron interrupts, "Lives have been saved, for what?"

The temperature has dropped. They knock back three, four, five more vodkas. His movements are controlled and his presence strangely chilled. Light-headed from too much drink, from weeks of craving close companionship, an absurd giddiness sweeps through her body. His eyes lock onto hers. She smiles sheepishly, too drunk to think of Sindy. He must have moved nearer, because his warm breath purls on her cheek.

He stands up and, as rigid as a tin soldier, marches back and forth across the room. "I-I'm sorry," he stammers. "I need to get this off my chest."

"What—?"

He cuts her off immediately. "I want to get to know you better." His tone is earnest, but the words are so clichéd he sounds comic. "Come."

Led by his hand, she follows. He pulls the cords dangling by a bedroom window and the blinds fall like eyelids.

She fills her lungs.

"Not now." He swings her onto his bed as though he has grown accustomed to getting what he wants.

The ceiling spins. Vodka is pungent on his breath. Sandwiched between the duvet and his body weight, her dress damp with alcohol, she feels the ticking of his heart, his kisses.

Her skin shouts, building to a crescendo, nerve ends screaming. *Don't touch me!*

"No," she manages. "I can't. Please, don't."

"Xolile, I want you."

She wipes oily sweat from her neck. "I haven't any condoms," words stumble from her mouth. "I'm not on the pill."

An incredulous look flits across his face.

"Shouldn't you use a condom?" she says.

"Relax," he replies. He smothers her with kisses.

Say no. Push him off.

He swings her like a ragdoll across the bed.

"Get undressed," he says.

There is rustling. He must be removing his jeans. Unbalanced and abruptly, she gets herself upright on the corner of the bed. He pulls off his shirt. The mound of flesh that is his stomach bulges over his G-string. Should she run, would he grab her?

135

Her rage burns and yet she is frozen, mannequin-stiff.

He begins dancing, slowly, leering, raising his arms in the air in a disturbing show of flirtation. He dips and sways, mimicking a belly dancer.

"Here, let me help." He unbuttons her dress.

She can only move sluggishly. The buttons she refastens are not aligned with the correct hole. Her mind detaches from her body. "No," she murmurs. Then louder, "*No!*"

"Come on, black cunt."

He slips his hands into her knickers and quickly pulls them down. Pushing her legs apart, his cock nuzzles the soft skin at the top of her thigh. His arms coil ivy-like around her waist. Her heart feels wrong. She has forgotten how to breathe. He forces the whole of his length into her. This is all of him. All his body seems to be in her – in her, around her. His hands under her back, his chest, his face above. Tense, clenched. Panting. His movements, a rash of violent jerks. She gasps – a short sharp breath of shock, then lies perfectly still.

Twisting his head to the ceiling, desperately he shudders. He whimpers strangely. And when he has finished and withdrawn, he turns aside, as though by moving from her, he can distance himself from what he has done.

She feels tattered, beaten up. She rolls to the edge of the bed on sheets damp with his pungent animal scent. He entwines his legs with hers. Then he is kissing her again. Her head tilts back, mouth open, gasping. This time her arms and legs thrash in an instinctive violent struggle.

She wrenches herself free, creeps to the bathroom. Vomits. Steals through the kitchen.

He dozes beneath the duvet. She salvages and tugs on underwear, the alcohol-splattered dress. Finds a blanket on the divan, burrows into a heap of cushions. Drifts in and out of consciousness, until daylight trickles into the room.

*

When she awakes fully, her body is moulded into cushions beneath a blanket on the kitchen floor. She is dreadfully hungover. She unlocks the glass door, drapes her arms, taut and trembling, over the verandah rail. The sky, a frigid silver sheet, is touched with apricot-yellow. Swallows swoop and ghost about the eaves.

Her mosquito bites itch as she stumbles inside. In his bedroom, Cameron has thrown the duvet back and sleeps, legs outstretched. Staring at him in disbelieving silence, she steps around his bed. Acrid smoke from smouldering fires sneaks through an open window.

Yawning, "Who's there?" he extends one arm. "Hey, it's you, shame." He chuckles, playfully sarcastic, and his unshaven chin juts presumptuously forwards.

In the kitchen, naked but for a knee-length sarong, he slips sunglasses on; brews coffee in a mocha pot. Does he know what he has done? The damage inflicted is like a gag.

She sinks into the divan and into the depths of mysterious clouds, grey shades of sadness. But the trauma is hers alone.

"I'm going to Mbabane," she says.

Cameron glances at her over a shoulder. She wants to smash his face in. She should report him. But no country is exempt from injustices towards women reporting rape.

The smoky, nutty coffee aroma assaults her nostrils. She cannot drink. Her throat is closed. He pushes his dark glasses further up the bridge of his nose. She is reflected in miniature.

He drives them onto the highway. He is wearing the signatory neck-scarf, the tail tucked into his shirt. She pokes her head outside the Land Rover, breathes in crisp morning air. When she winds the window up, she is trapped in a glass jar. From the other side, Xolile's face stares in through moving scenery – an approximation of herself in a parallel universe. The sun and moon glare at each other. Day and night. Give and take. Love and hate. Cold sweat drips down her spine. He brought his hurt out onto her. If he can do that, what might he do to Gift? Chills run through her body. Fists clenched, she flattens herself into the seat.

Mbabane nestles into one side of a green basin, backed by distant indigo mountains. Cattle are being driven from the over-grazed slopes. The rains have yet to begin; the earth is tempered and trampled, new shoots are scarce amongst the muted tones of weathered grass, the burnt stubble of winter. He drives through the rocky gully; immense slabs of stone overhang the road. Many are blackened on top as though burned by the sun. Others, huge, heavy and rotund, form whole mountainsides; all that is visible from the road is their orange belly. Has the land been raped too?

Sunlight flashes on a rear-view mirror. The shanty-type shacks of mud, wattle, corrugated metal, flash before her eyes; a man brandishing a knobkerrie. Had she acted quickly, could she have intervened? She hates the texture of the silence, that mysterious skin galvanising rock faces. The voiceless flesh of the land. And the sun's watery light.

In the spitting shower, she notices a pimpled patch below her left hip. She has read somewhere the incubation period for full-blown AIDS can be up to nine years. *Be rational. The virus will not yet show in tests.* But her judgement wavers and the dread of infection spreads a numbness to her fingers and toes. HIV is associated with promiscuity and dark sexual acts. The epidemic that plagues the black race. The Black Death. The hideous shame of contaminated blood. Unprotected sex.

This blemish is the first sign. Night sweats and nightmares are a sign too. Even sneezing can be a symptom. Make-up bleeds from her eyes. Xolile can wipe the tears from that face. But she can't wipe away the rage.

The past pulls. She had grown to love the valley; the peace, the solitude is part of herself and as the mist rose on a late summer's morning, wondered how she could leave. In winter, the river, turbid from rain, became a muddy colour. In spring its music swelled when the purple-pink of foxgloves leaned out across the water. The cottage is a casket of memories. Like an old companion, constant through happy days or days filled with sadness.

CHAPTER FIVE

Sunlight, spliced by the bars, spills across the blue kitchen linoleum like a smile emerging across the lips of a long-lost friend. The fridge is bare but for mouldy fingerprints. She goes to the pantry; a few tins are stacked in the vegetable rack. She opens cupboards. Empty shelves stare back. The bedsitting room feels familiar, yet different. Xolile ghosts past. Skin strokes skin. She hovers in the archway. Perches on the windowsill like a caged canary.

"Xolile! Xolile!" a voice shouts.

She opens the bedsit door.

Rachel's face glows. "I've seen your father's little mother," she gasps, out of breath from the three flights of stairs. "In other words, my mother's younger sister." She adds breathlessly, "Your great-aunt."

Rachel unbuttons her navy cotton jacket, beneath is the red and violet polka-dot dress she wore when they first met. Koliwe hugs her aunt, offers an uncertain smile, and is kissed on resentful lips in a performance of domineering vivacity.

Koliwe asks, "Tea?" then shrinks to the kitchenette. Returning, she sets down a tray with teacups and a plate of biscuits on the trestle table for her aunt.

"I'm making a family gathering for you," Rachel declares.

Reason should return with this obstinate aunt. But Koliwe's face is long and her voice quavers, "A party, for me?"

Rachel runs her forefinger along the row of Russian dolls. "*Hey*, but these are so, so perfect." Carefully, she resettles the wooden figures, each a receptacle for happiness, joy; pain – inside their protective mother. Rachel whirls like wind and fire combined, inspecting the furniture, bending to lift the corners of the sun-bleached checked cloth and revealing the collapsible table. She arranges cushions on the settee to show the respect an older woman is due. Reclining on the seat, her full lips clinging to a cigarette, perspiring and ebullient, Rachel has made herself at home. While her breathing calms, she scrapes at something stuck to her jacket lapel. "You *must* meet *everyone*."

Koliwe slumps down close to Rachel, plain and insubstantial beside her aunt's thickset limbs.

Rachel munches mechanically on a biscuit. She removes one of her sandals to examine varicose veins on the arch of her foot. "The family has a sacrificial spear," she announces.

There is an uncomfortable silence, broken by Rachel's chomping. "A cow was selected from a kraal – killed, skinned and eaten then and there."

"When and where?" Koliwe asks.

"Our homestead. Umcombotsi beer was brewed," Rachel continues vehemently. "The slaughter was for the ancestors, you see. The kraal's where the ancestors' presence is strong."

Koliwe struggles between coolness and irritation. "A *cow* was sacrificed?"

Rachel nods.

"But why?"

"We're living with our ancestors," Rachel counters, with a sly, pernicious look.

"You mean our ancestors are everywhere?"

"I'm remembering umcombotsi was poured into the ground for the ancestors to drink."

Koliwe pours the tea. Sacrifice is futile. Horrific. A resolution for them, but not for her. Her losses are not assuaged, not appeased. Does she belong to her father's family? Why has this woman sought her out? Rachel chatters on like a forest bird, steeped in traditions she will not share.

"You're seen as your father's daughter," Rachel explains.

That is how Koliwe is identified by other people.

"It won't be unusual to keep seeing Moses," Rachel continues, kicking off her other sandal. "You might hear someone calling your name."

Koliwe is a joke. A stupid joke to be poked at, made fun of. Tears held back overflow and at last she weeps.

Rachel gives a puzzled look. She caresses her niece. "Don't cry, my child. The ancestors are responsible for any bad things happening to you. You *must* visit a seer. Today, at Mahlanya." Rachel wipes the wetness from Koliwe's cheek.

Koliwe says, "See a seer?" with a mixture of scepticism and curiosity.

Rachel's tone is cautionary, "Moses' contempt for traditional beliefs caused his death." She dips forwards to stub out the cigarette, slides another from the packet in her handbag, lights it, shapes her mouth into an 'O' and puffs out cheeks as pliable as dough. Perfectly formed smoke rings plume, then dissolve between her painted lips.

Rachel cranes aside, half-whispering, "Your name's not Koliwe, it's Xolile, isn't it?" She kneads the smouldering tip of her cigarette into the ashtray, having hardly smoked it. Lights another, tilts her head back, and puffs.

Squirming into the cushions, guilty and inept, Koliwe stretches a hand across her face covering one eye. The tea tastes bitter. The room becomes dull and quiet. Koliwe and her aunt sip steaming Rooibos tea.

Rachel forces her feet into her sandals, stubs out the cigarette, belches, and rises to depart. "Come, Xolile. You must see the King's residence," she says, as they descend the stairs. She heads for a sleek and shining silver Mercedes Benz. Inside, Koliwe dabs her forehead, fans her face. Wearing an expansive smile, Rachel takes the highway towards Manzini. Koliwe, wiping sweat and tears from her face, searches for an excuse to turn back. Her father's voice drifts through the air: *A restless spirit. A final resting place.* The blue band of the Mdzimba Mountains lies in front.

"Mdzimba is sacred," Rachel is saying. "It is a sacred place." Smoke from villages swirls in the wind like strands of grey hair. Rachel does not point at Mdzimba with her finger, but uses her fist. She says women can only go so near to these burial places; Xolile cannot go where her father's grave should be. "You must stay in Swaziland. Your family's your roots."

They cross the small Usutu River. Lozita, the King's village, a beige-coloured expanse of buildings, dominates the horizon.

Rachel talks relentlessly and drives with immense determination. "That's the Houses of Parliament, where they make and break the laws. Xolile, this is a mountain coming up. There's a gorge, a gully, running here," she adds. "It's forested, see. They bury the kings in caves over there."

Rachel has drawn up on the red sandy soil of a filling station forecourt. "We're at Mahlanya. That means the place of madness."

Koliwe peers through the windscreen. Her aunt swaggers through a higgledy-piggledy arrangement of forklift trucks, articulated lorries, monstrous four-wheel drive land cruisers.

Returning minutes later, Rachel mops sweat from her forehead. "Here, all the people are mad, they selling you everything."

"They *try* to sell you everything. Do you have directions?" Koliwe asks.

"Just follow this track."

The Mercedes jolts along a dirt track, expelling dusty scarlet plumes. The air conditioning is not functioning, or Rachel has not thought to switch it on, and the Mercedes is as hot as a baker's oven. Koliwe glances at her watch. Already it is two o'clock.

They cruise through a shady banana grove. Pass four children chewing yellow sticks of cane sugar, slumped against a metal table offering for sale cheap soap bars, oranges, apples. A girl holds out a large, dark green avocado.

Rachel halts the car. "Sis, sawubona," she says to the girl. "Ngifuna kubona sangoma?"

Koliwe listens to the language she cannot understand.

"Utawubuya kusengakahlwi. Noma utambona nga Lesibili

ekuseni," the girl replies.

Irascible in the heat, Rachel screeches, "Cha, singeke simmele kute kube nguleso sikhatsi!" She throws up her arms, turns to Koliwe. "The sangoma's on a consultation. Back at eight, Tuesday." She inclines her head towards a compound of mud huts. "That's where the seer lives." She rams the Mercedes into gear and sets off for Mbabane in an angry outburst of dust.

CHAPTER SIX

A sudden urge to retrieve her belongings from Cameron's bungalow chokes up inside. When she drives down the mountainside, fields are being weeded, crops have started to grow from the deep russet-red earth. Boys walk towards Lobamba carrying bundles of branches to build the king's kraal for the Incwala ceremony.

It is a bright cloudy morning. The sun sits high above Cameron's bungalow. The guard unlocks the gates. She parks in the courtyard. The heat is fierce. Nothing moves. The static garden is a snapshot of lethargy. She had intended leaving the office early, but Cameron had pestered her with errands. No matter how hard she tries to bury incensed demons, they surface spitefully.

She opens the car door. Barking, ears alert, the Alsatians bound across the lawn; they break into a trot when they recognise her, then flop down on the paving stones. The silky material of her peach-coloured dress with small yellow flowers has been cut well, falls nicely. She walks self-consciously across the courtyard. Will Cameron be furious or apologetic? Framed by the kitchen window, a young woman is seated at the sideboard drinking coke. The thin straps of her top show her creamy shoulder blades, tanned, slightly inflamed from exposure to the sun. She hurls Koliwe a stony stare with fearless blue flames for eyes. The ground rushes away. Koliwe is shrivelling into a tiny ball.

"*You're* Koliwe?" Sindy, raising her dainty pointy chin, turns and disappears into Cameron's bungalow.

The sky is liquid mercury with black clouds weighted with water. Loneliness hangs about the empty cottage at the end of the garden. Envelopes the verandah, clasps cold arms around her. Three windows are hostile holes. She scrubs an oval-shape on the grimy glass.

Back in the bungalow, the kitchen ceiling is misted with rising steam; an aroma of lamb chops fried with rosemary wafts from a pan and Rose's warbling voice ripples around the room. Rose is singing a hymn, while stirring a pan of boiling rice for the dogs. She stares at Koliwe with open contempt. Her toes poke through holes in her shoes. Her face contorts as though she has taken a dose of foul medicine when Koliwe asks if Cameron is in.

"Let me help you dry the dishes, then you can show me where to put them," Koliwe suggests, unsure of the status of their relationship.

Rose glares at her. "Can't speak siSwati, can you, Mama?"

Koliwe tries another approach. "Mr Cameron said your boyfriend works in the mines?"

Rose repeats, "Boyfriend works in the mines," in a mincing voice.

"You visit him in South Africa?"

Rose's eyes glass over.

Koliwe asks where Nathi and Queenie have gone.

Chewing gum, Rose's jaw works lazily. She says, in a la-di-da tone, "They went to a sangoma. Sangoma said bad blood run through their body."

"They should get treatment at a medical centre," Koliwe says. "You can take me to them, please."

Rose eyes Koliwe's hand-tailored frock – a garment the maid could never afford – and makes a snide remark in siSwati. She never grudges Cameron, a foreign white man, giving orders, but she does not fancy receiving orders from a foreign black woman. "Mr Cameron says you left."

Taking up her cases, Koliwe nods.

Rose resumes singing then stops. "Jesus!" she shrieks, throwing up her hands. "I forget hospital appointment." She hurries past the sleeping dogs to leave by the laundry room.

Cameron's face pokes through the doorway. He wears a severe disciplinary look. His eyebrows have knotted together. "Hello, what do you want?"

Koliwe's face is crumpled by emotions she only half understands. As Cameron retreats, she follows him outside.

The sliding garage door is bunched up like a concertina. Safe from the sun's glare, the guard slouches against the Land Rover. Cameron thrusts a roll of Rand notes into his hand then gestures for the man to make himself scarce. The Alsatians' paws clatter on the granite paving slabs as they slink towards their master. He bends low, viewing her from the dogs' perspective. He clicks his fingers. Three pairs of eyes stare coolly in Koliwe's direction.

"What are you doing here?" he asks.

Xolile cannot connect with him on any level. Could she ever? An intense contempt for him crawls across her skin.

"What do you want?" he snaps.

Her confrontation had been unprepared. "Aren't you forgetting something? Didn't we have a friendship?"

"Friendship?"

She rolls her eyes to say *of course*. She has seen that look of surprise mixed with hatred before. She should have known this exchange would be futile and shabby. Did what they have constitute a friendship, even in her eyes? "Can we talk?"

His words are as blunt as a hammer, "*Talk?* What is there to *talk* about? Your time here's over." He stomps back to the kitchen, arms flailing, as though wallowing through a thick swamp, thrashing between triumph and despair.

Returning to the office late afternoon, she finds Cameron's canteen tray and lunch debris on her desk. He is checking the answering machine for messages.

"Be a darling," he says, "take my tray to the catering hatch, stack it on one of the trolleys." His eyes hold a hint of cruelty.

Nervously, she blinks at the remnants of a tomato sandwich, flesh, pips and bread crusts, camouflaged by a crumpled, beer-soaked paper serviette.

"Take the tray to the catering hatch. Stack it for me."

She wants to answer. The distance between them is immense. She is unmoored in time and place. She scans the project proposal on her computer screen. He carries on with his business. Speaking to him now would be like trying to converse with a void. Her legs transport her down to the canteen with his lunch tray.

She heads to the washrooms by way of the stairs, sticks two fingers down her throat and vomits the lunch she had eaten into the toilet bowl.

When she returns, the cruelty in his eyes remains, reminding her of a schoolteacher from the past.

"I'm in a hurry. I've a flight to London this evening," he explains.

As he passes, in an insidious effort to distress her, his foot kicks her chair leg, jolting her forwards.

"Hey, I'm off to Incwala tomorrow. Wanna come?" Maureen's voice sounds nasal and affected on the telephone.

Koliwe mulls the invitation over. "Okay, let's meet at half-ten."

Compared to Oxford, Mbabane is the size of a postage stamp. She crosses it in a matter of minutes. There is no real city centre, just a development of shopping precincts, the Mall and the new Swazi Plaza. The Plaza is crowded with hustlers and hawkers, offering goods ranging from children's sweets to the latest expensive perfumes. She spots Maureen seated on a kerb beside a battered Cressida.

"Incwala's held at Lobamba, capital of the Swazi nation." In the sand, Maureen traces the route with her forefinger.

Koliwe remembers the boys flocking to the grounds. She squats at Maureen's side. "Why there?"

"Because Lobamba's the king's main residence. The country's ritual centre," Maureen says. "Why, you've lost your shine! Something wrong?"

Koliwe picks at her well-worn denim jeans; through a hole pokes the nut-brown skin of her knee. She shrugs at Maureen, and grunts guardedly.

"I see it on your face," Maureen says. "Open up."

She cannot reply, and sits in silence watching the birds despondently, eyes glazed like a plastic doll's.

Maureen clears papers from the Cressida's front seat. Koliwe clambers in. Heat shimmers above the tarmac as they pass concrete houses, tiny and forlorn, that straggle up mountains and hillsides. Jojo birds perched on the telephone poles dotted along the road take to the air; they flap alongside the car for a short way then scatter, their glossy black tail feathers trailing like streamers against the blue sky.

Palm trees line the long, straight highway leading to the site – a grassy plain near Lobamba – the blue Mdzimba Mountains form a backdrop. Cattle huddle beneath the few acacia trees for shade. The men preparing for the ceremony in a gigantic cluster, wear scarlet feather head-dresses and loin cloths cut from leopard and impala pelts. Coarse cattle tails, tied just below the bicep, flow down each warrior's right forearm. Twisted strips of cow skin stretch from shoulder to waist. A trumpet is sounding when they arrive, the shrill notes crash through the warriors' cacophony. Maureen sets off on foot, then vanishes into the throng. Skirting the herd, and intent on giving the warriors a wide berth also, Koliwe follows. A stench of sweat and cow dung closes around her. Taking a deep breath, she barges into the jostling army. She has to force her way through a sea of sturdy sticks and shields of taut ox hide. One warrior prods her with a knobkerrie. Fear flares up her spine. Some glower, others avert their eyes, while in their midst a cow licks her calf with slow, laborious strokes.

Koliwe bursts from discomfort into white sunlight. The Sibaya, a circular wooden palisade, serves as an amphitheatre for the great annual ceremony. Rondavels are arranged in clutches around the edges.

Maureen has cut through the warriors to avoid the locals teeming into the central area. Her voice leaks through the warriors' din. "The Sibaya," she shouts over her shoulder, "was used in the past to keep lions from the cattle. Incwala is danced inside. It's a national prayer the ancestors must experience."

Rows of slatted benches are reserved as prime viewing for tourists. Maureen finds a place for them to sit, opposite Colonel Johnston, in the stalls. The colonel wears a white jacket, white shorts and white safari hat. Mrs Johnston's face is eclipsed by a voluminous straw hat.

Women strut through the main entrance, many naked from the waist up, bare breasts bobbing, skin shimmering with crystalline sand specks. Their lurid armlets, necklaces of porcupine quills, clay and glass beads, wink in the sunlight. They move as a single entity, grass skirts swaying in time to the rhythmic thud of drums. Vividly coloured ties are bound around their waists; a white band crosses each brow; their hair is combed into neat beehive-shapes. Dust clouds sparkle and glitter, churned up by knee-high kicks, as they move in a muddled mass, their grouping as disordered as Koliwe's emotions. The chaos increases when the warriors enter, then the women shrink to one side. There is endless gruff chanting and shuffling in sun-baked sand. The men's garish red feather headdresses flutter, their cloaks of cattle tails swish, as they assemble into lines.

"They're forming regiments according to age," Maureen says.

There is no shelter from the sun or Incwala's turbulence. Koliwe's head throbs; the skin around her eyes wrinkles from squinting. She rests her elbows on her knees and cups her chin in her hands. The warriors prance and leap energetically, hurling themselves up to the strength of the sun, plummeting into soft sun-baked sand. They shake and stomp, fingers a-flutter like butterfly wings, and the seeds of emafahlawane tied about their ankles rattle in time to the drums. The dancing grows in intensity. Dust rises in a thigh-high mist. Their cries swell; crescendo. The array of sticks they hold clash together to form a wooden screen.

"That's the sacred enclosure, inhlambelo," Maureen says, pointing at a corral to one side of the arena built of sturdy logs and wattle. "Once the bull's killed, the tail and skin are placed there, and the king is smeared with special medicines."

Koliwe's fingers comb curls, a nail snags on a strand. "There's Cameron!" she exclaims.

Cameron walks briskly from a cool drinks stand. He does not acknowledge Maureen or Koliwe, then he is lost in a squall of people and dust. Suspicion shines in the whites of Koliwe's eyes, as she slides her feet from her sandals. Why isn't he on his way to London?

Maureen pokes Koliwe mischievously. "You'll be the only person here who hasn't slept with him." She pauses, then emits a hollow chuckle ripe with scorn. "Apart from Phepile."

Koliwe sits stock still, as though shackled to the slats. Her skin feels cold and moist. She wipes perspiration from her forehead.

Maureen gives a hurried, worried look. "He's treating you alright?"

"No..." her voice wavers, unsure whether to confide. "He's not who I thought he was."

"Did anything happen between you?"

There is no coherent thread to Koliwe's thoughts. The sun is blindingly hot. The dancing, frenzied. She scoops up a handful of dirt. She wants to be at peace with the earth passing between her fingers. She questions Maureen more about the ceremony.

"Tomorrow there'll be a repeat performance."

Is Incwala a spectacle, for tourists, she wonders, as the dancers disperse? Does it keep traditional beliefs alive? An exotic exhibit from a shadowy, half-imagined past? Whatever the ceremony was, or is becoming, like her it is in a transitional state.

This is the golden hour. The sky is indigo splashed with papaya. A flock of birds glides overhead, their amber bellies touched by the setting sun. Palm trees cast tall shadows over the main drive as they cruise in a queue of clapped-out vehicles. Koliwe tilts the sunshield; the bite in the air makes her shiver. A medley of clouds plays until a veil of indigo, studded with stars, creeps across the sky. The magic of Incwala gone, the roaming crowds' focus is on the night ahead in town.

CHAPTER SEVEN

Voices from the back-office drift through the air. Phepile is saying she heard Thandi had moved near to Usutu. Gliding to Koliwe's desk, fiercely, Phepile says, "Why not check Thandi's homestead? Someone there will know Thandi's address."

Koliwe swings the Mazda from the parking space. Sunlight strikes the white fronts of small square houses. There is a raw gleam from a pile of aluminium cans outside a bottle shop, where men congregate to listen to township music on the radio. She extracts one two-hundred Emalangeni note from her back pocket, as she draws up on the forecourt of a Caltex garage amidst a herd of goats. Strains of Afrikaans Boere musiek filter into the car and a young black man runs across the forecourt.

"I'll have eight hundred rand of ninety-five," Koliwe says to him.

Women serve at a canteen hatch. A packet of biltong lies on the counter. She scans the shelf of cigarettes. Glances over her shoulder at the white woman behind her, selects Marlboro. Her fingers move over the serrated edges of coins in her pocket. Stepping forwards, the woman callously elbows Koliwe, and picks up a strip of biltong – dried beef wrapped in plastic, as tough and wizened as the woman's expression. Koliwe buys the cigarettes, trudges back to the car under the sun's brazen face. A couple of forecourt attendants wash her windscreen. They are outside, looming over her privileged life. Stalking in the shadows are her fears, ready to spring out at any moment. Sometimes they overcome her. Some days, life in general. All places. All people. All things. Through the soap-smeared windscreen, she makes out the woman with her biltong, conversing with a ginger-blonde teenaged boy who loafs beside a four-by-four, a gun holster prominent on his waist. The boy has a stolid oblong body, the shoulders of an ox. With his sturdy walking boots, thick socks, khaki shorts and shirt, he is dressed like an

Afrikaner farmer's son. After all, there have been a lot of farm killings going on.

Sucking nicotine in, she pulls away from the filling station. The armed boy has not moved. She winds down the window, lets out the smoke, tears onto the highway and the boy's and the woman's forms reduce in the mirror to dots.

Sprinting down a side-track is a child. She waves a newspaper at Koliwe, flagging her down from the sandy verge. Flies swarm around the girl's eyes. The gaping mouth blotted with sun shapes merges into Thandi's unforgettable face. Koliwe snatches the newspaper through the window, chucks a handful of coins at the child, then clamps the folded newspaper beneath an arm. "Hey," she calls to the little girl, "d'you live nearby?"

"Yes, that way." With a proud gesture the child points back the way she had come.

"Do you know a girl called Thandi?"

The child's face brightens. "I used to sell scones with Thandi."

"Where's Thandi now?"

"She was taken, by a man."

"What did he look like?"

"He looked like a white man," the girl replies.

"Anything else you can say about him?"

"Thandi told me he said everything will be alright and he'll pay Thandi's school fees."

"Thandi lived up the hill?"

"Yes, Thandi used to live there."

Small beehive-shaped rondavels, surrounded by reed fences, are spaced along the dust track leading through the mountains. Koliwe urgently scans the missing persons sections, then drives despondently across a plateau sprinkled with wattle and thorn bushes.

A buzzard soars over mauve mountaintops, hovers, fixed against the blue canvas of sky. How can the bird be motionless in mid-air? Then the buzzard dives, disappearing behind the ridges. Staring after the bird in disbelief and into a hazy and tragic past, Koliwe halts the car, unable to take it in. Heat shimmers above the grasses; the air scorches. Although the atmosphere is sultry and the sky a dull bluish-yellow, there is a softness to the light, as there had been *that* afternoon. This is the place with the lone homestead. Ahead, backed by the rugged mountains' rocky ridges, is the squatter farm, small and distant, nestling in a valley.

The wild beauty of the landscape near Thandi's hut now holds a distrubing portent of disaster. The overgrown dirt path leads uphill through scrub. She shivers, slipping from the Mazda and onto a sweep of sandy grassland stippled with tyre marks and cloven hoof prints. Sunlight scurries through the grasses, painting them gold. The homestead is deserted. Uncared for. Tall weeds and thistles obscure the path to the door. Something holds her from knocking on the dented corrugated iron.

Her shadow lengthens into a long black train. The darkness sucks her in. The fetid stench of fermented fruit and wine vinegar makes her choke. A lizard scuttles close to her foot, jade smooth and shiny black; its tongue flicks from its mouth. Sunlight slips through chinks in the walls, a splintered window shutter. The room houses sacks of sugar, shrivelled cabbages. Spinach leaves are stashed against one wall. On the floor is a grass sleeping mat and a lumpy-looking mattress stained with blotches like brown clouds. Swift as lightning, the lizard streaks up the door.

Outside, the sun is blisteringly hot. Inside is cool and dark. She roots through heaps of darned dresses, tangled headscarves, tattered scraps too far gone to be mended. Even peers under the mattress. Have the police been here? Have they, too, raked through this clutter of cottonwool and scented creams? Have they rummaged through drawers that horde plastic bottles? Her eyes smart, her nose wrinkles at the pervasive perfume of cheap scent and potent body odour.

155

The door creaks closed. Wispy grasses stroke her shins and crackle underfoot. The sun, now an amber disc, reflects off the wing mirror, glaring like a warning signal. Red-black dots dance, uncontrolled, obscuring a girl's face. The man dashes from the shack. Two silhouettes dissolve into the valley. The sun behind screams, making long shadows slide. The clunk as wood strikes bone. Everything goes fuzzy. The man whips round like a whipping top and runs.

The ground becomes rougher, the grasses thinner. Is this the spot Thandi was killed? In stillness, Koliwe listens to the air and the descending dusk. Listens for a silenced heart.

CHAPTER EIGHT

After scrubbing sticky circles inside cupboards, sweeping and washing the floor, wiping the dusty wardrobe, the bed-sit remains drab and grimy. She is invisible, sliding in between Mbabane's high-rise concrete offices and apartments, through sandy streets, confined alleyways, across the market to the clinic. Bars of morning sunlight and dark blocks of shade fall across pavements.

The crimson sky is mesmerising. Cameron is disgusting. He has duped her. Infected her. Used her. How *could* she have been so stupid? Is she a coward or crazy? Volts of fury shoot through her veins.

Will she remain inextricably bound to him for her entire life? Will she die HIV positive? Because of him? Where is Thandi? Who is the girl Cameron keeps at his lodge? Is she there against her will?

Despairing nurses spend months, years, trying to persuade clients to test. She has seen the fear in the eyes of women who carry a fatal virus. The test paper announces their fate: one strip for negative; two strips for positive. She has heard the doctor's spiel about the regularity with which antiretroviral medicines must be taken.

Automatic doors open onto the reception area's yellowed walls; a ceiling fan rattles like helicopter blades churning the stagnant disinfectant odour. Prickly heat aggravates her neck. Her skin is damp with beads of worry. Scores of eyes blink white from the blackness of over-crowded clinic corridors. Her mind goes back through months of moving through similarly over-crowded spaces. Rows of clients on up-turned Coca-Cola crates. Cartons of disposable gloves, sealed test kits, boxes of syringes. The probing questions asked: When did you last have sex? How many partners in the last year? How do you protect yourself? She understands the importance of knowing her status. Knows the catchphrases on brochures word for word: *ABC. Abstain. Be Faithful. Condomise.* One woman's face is familiar. Those wide-set eyes, the heart-shaped face smothered with blisters. The woman coughs violently. Koliwe returns in her mind to the countryside – a heavenly blue sky, the green envy of the river.

The mandatory counselling session is abrupt. The nurse is also the pre-test counsellor. She closes the treatment room door, the soapy smell wafting from her hands. The white plastic chair is hard. Koliwe feels accosted by the HIV and AIDS posters – a helpless development worker contaminated with guilt.

The nurse asks whether she has tested before. "The window for testing is three months. You're certain that period's over? Then a test for HIV antibodies can be taken."

Beneath waves of fear, Koliwe is submerged. The room skews and groans. A strange sick horror lodges in her stomach. Xolile, a silent living ghost.

The nurse snaps on latex gloves; her tired eyes focus on the syringe; cheeks bulge as she talks about adjusting to living positively. "You have a husband? Steady partner? According to statistics," the nurse says, "new HIV infections are most likely to occur in married women, or women with a steady partner. Here we use a rapid test. Results are obtained within minutes. We must place a drop of blood on this strip."

Koliwe uncurls her balled fists. Seconds later her blood has coursed along the test kit bars. The assault in Cameron's house happened only three weeks ago. How could she have overlooked that?

"I think I've mixed up the dates," she admits.

"This here," the nurse points at the calendar on her desk, "divides weeks into days. The year into months." She shoots Koliwe a condescending look. "When was the *last* date you had unprotected sex?" she stresses.

"Probably three weeks ago."

"Return when you've worked out the dates."

"May I have the result?"

A long moment of agony passes.

"It will be inaccurate," the nurse says. The nurse's steely eyes say some experiences cannot be left behind. Some nightmares follow you into daylight. She knows what these men are like. "You could be highly infectious."

Koliwe attempts to gather herself together. Is she living positive? Is Cameron? Did someone see her at the clinic before or after the test? The nurse must have deduced from her English accent that she is an overseas aid worker. Must think her a fool.

She moves through dirty sunlight, anger beating in her chest. The pace is fast on Fridays. The dark mass blocking the bedsit entrance separates into two figures; one tall and lean; one squat and broad. Sergeant Lolo and his assistant? Have they news of Thandi? Hadn't Cameron intimated she avoid the police at all costs? She puts her head down, walks through crowds. Dashes into the empty hall, up the staircase. Calls, "Hello! Hello!" scurries downstairs and into an alley. Cut across Allistair Millar Street to Mbabane's disjointed hub. Could the policemen have dissolved into the broad, leafy streets? The footpaths that straggle up mountains and hillsides?

She takes the envelope from her pigeonhole, opens it. The letterhead reads:

Francis Callow, Director, U.K Aid, Southern Africa Branch.

Dear Koliwe,

I want to clarify how we see your progression within the charity and to discuss the terms and conditions of your appointment.

Francis Callow's door is shut. She raps below his name on the wooden plaque.

He calls, "Come in," in a sing-song voice.

A computer buzzes therapeutically on a smoked glass desk. Everything in his office is slick and glossy, except the man himself, who is balding and has a strained viscous face. His thinning hair matches his camel-coloured suit. Spectacles magnify his green eyes and occupy the upper region of his face. Sideburns, the colour of burnt caramel, conceal his cheeks.

"Koliwe! We meet, at last!" he exclaims, eyes widening. "I had *so* wanted to be here when you arrived. What with my absence, then our London director relocating, there's been staff shortages. Lots to catch up on."

His office is aggressively hot. Photographs stacked neatly beside his computer, labelled 'Magazine Shots', carry stock images of poverty-stricken refugees, pitifully thin babies sprawled on hospital beds, a woman carrying a wheat crop bundle upon her head.

Mr Callow asks, "What's your progress since arriving?"

Reflecting on U.K Aid's food security projects, the survey on the regularity of repeat HIV tests, the boreholes and irrigation project, it is a struggle to define progress.

Mr Callow talks at length about U.K Aid's successes. "Your projects are coming together?"

"I've mainly been updating surveys, researching, and laying foundations for new development projects. But there is an existing infrastructure. If we put money into local hospitals and health centres, surely our efforts would be more effective, or at least better directed."

The man says, "Sorry, can't help there," with indifference.

"I can explain about the rust project in the sugar plantations," she says.

Mr Callow nods encouragement. "How are you getting on with Mr Cameron?"

"I've seen a good deal of him," she says icily. She looks across the reflective tabletop and into jaundiced, clouded eyes, of the snide, salty man.

"You're measuring the impact of short-term, emergency feeding programmes?"

The Santa Claus solution, she thinks. "Token gifts instead of long-term sustainable development work?"

"Your opinion may be worthy, accurate, even," he admits. "However, NGOs are *non*-governmental," he emphasises, and a smile of satisfaction spreads across his lips.

"And what about salaries?" She clenches her hands beneath the desk. She had heard Phepile and her other colleagues discussing this unfairness in the office. "I'd like to understand about the wage structure, why the black African women are paid less than white or black British staff." "Most blacks are born in Africa. You were born in England, that's why your salary's higher. But," he lolls back into his chair with a sardonic grin and, cupping a ginger-haired hand to his lips, subtly clears his throat, adding, "I don't see you as black." He looks into her restless eyes, *Oh, come on,* his expression seems to say. "It's never been better to be black," he replies in a quiet, jovial way.

Did he mean to be ambiguous?

He looks down at his desk; sandy-coloured lashes shield his eyes. "Wage structures within British Aid aren't determined by qualifications or experience, but by the financial market each employee's from. If you'd been born in, say, Rwanda, you'd earn less than a third of the salary of someone born in the U.K, even if you were more highly qualified." He massages his cheeks, burying his fingertips in bushy sideburns. "We are an equal opportunities employer. I take it you're not disputing that? I would strongly, *strongly* advise moderating your views. Consider your *future*, Koliwe – sorry, Xolile – you've much to gain, much to lose. It would be a tragedy to fall out with U.K Aid so early in your career."

Be reasonable. Unemotional. "What about my contract?" The question slips out before she has considered the consequences. "Is my position permanent?" Steeling herself for repercussions, she laces her fingers together on her lap.

Francis Callow mashes his fingers together on the desktop. "Cameron tells me you don't agree with our approach. You're a little –" he sticks his index fingers up and waggles them mid-air – 'difficult'."

The discussion has reached a crisis within a matter of minutes. There is a sullen silence. A young woman with twine-thin arms and legs enters the office holding two steaming cups of coffee. Sindy. Her sleek vanilla-blonde hair is tied in a bun. Rage flashes through Koliwe. Sindy puts one cup on a cork tile before her, the other in front of Francis Callow, and flounces out.

Mr Callow takes the coffee in great gulps. He seems to be waiting for Koliwe to speak.

Staring back at him, finally, she says, "The situation's desperate in some child-headed families. In December, I submitted a request for U.K Aid to fund one more support worker."

"Yes, yes. Look, my dear, we want you here. It's just" – he takes another gulp of coffee – "we'd rather you worked in South Africa."

"But I – I haven't..."

"Until now, I've been impressed by what I've heard," he says waspishly.

She watches him with a hostile fury, and says contemptuously, "Then why can't I stay here?"

Reclining into his swivel chair, he positions his chest towards her. He is quiet for a moment then says, "That wouldn't look good now, would it?"

Their eyes meet for a split second. A bilious hatred for Cameron flushes through her veins. This horrible room is boiling. Outside, a mass of rock veers towards the window, forests glissade down steep mountain slopes. Her emotions landslide too as she dwells upon the effect Cameron has had. But

162

the desire – a gravitational pull – to state her case seems absurd.

"In order to obtain your work permit, Cameron had to submit an application through the Ministry of Employment, explaining why a local person wasn't suitable. To have the application accepted, a small amount of cash was exchanged. Cameron had thought," Mr Callow adds irritably, "the whole thing was settled, but they're now insisting I employ *two* Swazi nationals as well." He taps the desktop with a pen. "I'm trying to decide what on earth to do about this." Running a hand through his light-brown mane, he emits a strained, "Ahem". His diction is clipped, each terse word pinched, "Sadly, your work here will be over shortly."

"But I want to stay."

"Nowadays, one year's the maximum in any one location, although my mantra's six months. You'll throw your career away if you stay too long. Your transfer to South Africa's in a couple of weeks. The way to move up in this business is to keep moving on."

She swallows sharply. "Then how does one gain an understanding of a country's problems?"

Francis Callow is shaking his head. Like England, he is grim, dreary, cold.

She tries another tack. "My contract here is for one year."

Cloaked in indifference, Francis Callow shrugs, and goes on with breezy detachment, "We're briefing your replacement."

The telephone rings.

"Hang on a minute, dear." He winks; lifts the receiver with one hand; the other hand waves Koliwe away like an annoying mosquito.

An old anger, like hunger, aches in her bones; a curious brooding anger bequeathed from father to daughter.

CHAPTER NINE

The stars grow faint in the depth of an arctic-blue night. Moonlight steals through gaps in the curtains, sneaking silver across the floor.

Koliwe feels stronger. Xolile hovers close by. Listening. But thinking of Cameron, guilt spreads ivy-like over Koliwe's skin. One moment from their drunken mating stands out. His bell-end flopping against her thigh. Disgust mingles with remorse. Had she initiated *it*? How to recover from the too-drunk-to-remember shame? If only she could dissolve like a handful of pills in water. Trembling with fury, she lies flat on her back, taking short shallow breaths. There is a scream deep inside where it cannot be heard by anyone. The venom congeals in her belly, and the shock of reality affects her so strongly, her whole body pulls away from the bed.

The Sunday silence is broken by the occasional barking of faraway dogs. She presses her foot on the accelerator. Within minutes, she is veering onto the highway towards Manzini. Determined to turn her life around. Take control. Driven by frustration, hurtling past the hustlers who mill around roadside stalls. The long distance to Lobamba passes in a flash of trees, houses, huts. She swerves onto the red dirt track she travelled with Rachel. Lines of sweat dribble down her sides. The chill of anger haunts her body. She looks to the purple mountains beyond the hills with hot, hateful eyes. The children she saw from Rachel's Mercedes stand in front of the stall, as before, sucking yellow sticks of sugar cane. Heat rages.

The Mazda bounces over the pumpkin-sized boulders bordering the seer's compound – a conglomeration of rusty metal sheds, mud-and-stick rondavels and single-storey brick houses arranged around a dusty yard. She slams the car door with hard precision and finds herself in front of four men in blue factory overalls, seated on a wooden bench outside one of the houses.

She storms through the spiky weeds. "Sangoma?" She gives each man her harshest stare, which three of them ignore. The one nearest the door, a man of skin and bone, rises and waves her in.

Books, piles of files, papers and pamphlets are scattered everywhere, cascading from shelves to lie in hopeless disorder around the feet of the puny, aged, unshaven man, seated in the shadow of a tall bookcase at right angles to a desk. He wears a red loin cloth beneath two small animal pelts; a matching cloth is draped diagonally across his torso from shoulder to waist.

She does not like his deeply creased face, swirling with patterns like the grain of aged wood. He grins; pouches crinkle under his eyes.

"Sangoma?" she asks.

Of course, the old man only speaks siSwati. His eyelids are like brown crepe paper fluttering as his eyes roll up to the ceiling, until all that is visible are the pinkish whites. The skin on the backs of his hands is taut. His long, bony fingers fumble through heaps of papers.

A wasted trip. It was ridiculous to have believed the answers to her troubles lay in this room with this old man. He sits in silence for a while, then gestures for her to leave. Swiftly striding through the doorway and into the brutal glare of the sun, Koliwe heads towards her car. But the man who waved her in grabs her arm.

"Now you see the sangoma," the man's voice is small and impassive. His nails cut into her flesh like razor blades.

He leads her through a complex pattern of mud huts, rondavels, concrete bungalows and between two rusty, decrepit barbed-wire fences, to a hut of mud and wattle set far from the other buildings and the brush line. "Here, wait outside," he says.

Leaving her stroking her sore arm, he disappears inside.

Reeds point out from the bottom of the rondavel's thatched roof, making an irregular fringe. Chunks are missing from the rooftop and grasses grow in a patchwork of odd clumps. Koliwe swipes at annoying flies darting from the thatch. Seconds later, the man comes out and walks a little way along the path. He halts Koliwe with his hand, indicating she should stay. She lingers indignantly. Presently a woman's face appears in the doorway. She beckons Koliwe.

Koliwe's hair is brushed by the uneven thatch. The air is stale and fusty. The only light, a silvered shaft, streams from a window set high in the wall inches below where the thatch begins, and above the woman now sitting cross-legged on a dusty, moth-eaten reed mat.

The woman puts a glass of water to her lips, half-closes her eyes and makes a long slurping sound. A black top hat conceals her forehead. Indigo and plum-coloured bruises with crisscross slits, the width of a razor-blade's cut, scar the skin beneath her cheekbones. Her bill-shaped nose reminds Koliwe of the storks that balance on one leg in the marshes. Pearl-white and aqua-blue beads are strung on the leather thongs around her fleshy ankles and wrists. Her bare feet have a waxy sheen, the ridged toenails toughened, dull. The woman nods. Koliwe nods too. Although the woman's skin resembles crumpled paper, Koliwe guesses they are about the same age. She is enthralled by the woman's enigmatic presence and her piercing ochre-yellow eyes; they hold a distinct quality of endless patience.

Between them lies a goatskin mat. Goat and sheep skulls hang on the walls; shawls, strings of beads. A shield, a spear and the King's face are printed on a maroon cape, attached with drawing pins to vertical wooden slats. A pestle and large granite mortar stand in one corner; peacock feathers rest in another, for calming the sky when it roars.

Koliwe says, "Sangoma?" expecting a reply in siSwati.

The woman answers, "Yes."

Relieved, Koliwe kneels on the mat. The sangoma indicates for Koliwe to remove her sandals. Nervously, she takes them off and places them by the doorway. Far-off noises of children playing float into the room; giggling voices, odd squeals of delight.

The woman reaches for the blue bag on a three-legged table beside her. The ends of the drawstring are frayed and grimy. "This," she says, indicating the bag, "is my sikhwama." She takes the sikhwama up, pours its contents onto the goatskin. Stones, dice, bones, rings, coins Koliwe does not recognise, pinky-white spiral shells, six gleaming silver balls, four opaque marbles tumble across the fur.

From the window a silver spear of sunlight slants across the sangoma's face as she scoops the collection up in her hands, pushes it into the sikhwama and passes Koliwe the bundle.

"Do I throw them down?" Koliwe asks.

"Shake them. Throw them onto the mat." The sangoma's voice has a velvety softness.

Koliwe is silent for a little. The sikhwama she cradles with meticulous care holds something mysterious and unanswerable.

By now the sun is an orange disc suspended in a pink sky. She glimpses the half-moon through the tiny window. Lizards shoot up and down the mud walls with the swiftness of arrows then, stopping stock-still, become tiny sculptures. Every so often, a lizard plummets to the floor with a soft plunk, or skits across the reed mat near to the sangoma's feet.

Koliwe jiggles the sikhwama in her hands. Delicately tips the base up to her stomach. Two marbles roll from the goatskin onto the mat. Three of the shiny metal balls glide across the floor into shadows; the other items drop to the fur with a light thud.

Slanting forwards in the slim ray of dark light falling from the window, gazing, unblinking, as though making a crucial penultimate move in an intricate chess game, the sangoma scrutinises the lie of bones inscribed with mysterious runes, smooth flat pebbles, dice, rings, burnished sovereigns, seashells.

She stops Koliwe, saying, "Something is holding you back. Someone in your past is stopping you from getting where you want to go." She uses her hands as feelers, as though travelling through passages of time. "You hear thunder rumbling. Birds disappearing forecasts lightning," the sangoma croons. "Children run happily into the rain, but elders say, *No. Fire and water. Thunder. Lightning. Rain. Danger. Run.*"

Darkness descends on the world outside; the circling flies settle. The little rondavel is peaceful. Through the tardy half-light, a face emerges in swirling froth and foam. The artist submerged in the river, clutching at reeds at the close of summer. If he sinks down, might he lie quietly? Find inner stillness?

The sangoma has drawn a cigarillo case from her dress pocket. She selects a cigarette. "He's saying you must talk to him. He's saying go into the past. To hear. In your mind there is knowing." There is a sheen to the waxy skin of the sangoma's arms from the fitful play of the candle she has already lit. "He's saying you mustn't blame."

"Who?"

"Yourself." The sangoma pauses. "What's your name?"

"Xolile."

"Xolile. Ah, yes. The One Who Forgives." The sangoma slips the cigarette between her lips, tilts forwards and lights it from the flickering flame. A transparent ribbon of grey smoke unfolds into the black air. As the sangoma contemplates Xolile's future, the smoke unravels, wafting to the highest regions of the thatched roof. "Take this." She places a circular plastic container the size of a two pence coin onto the reed mat. The top is yellow, the bottom red: Snuif is etched into the lid. "Put pinch on hand. Sniff." She sucks on the cigarette and sways to one side to dodge the smoke weaving a question mark around her head.

"Take snuff, listen. He'll tell you. You will hear."

Mosquitoes waltz around the doorway, performing complex abstract patterns. They invade the rondavel through the torn gauze curtains and whine around Xolile's head.

Smoke from between the sangoma's lips spirals upwards. Her dreamy eyes hold foresight. She places the snuff container on Xolile's palm. "You come for kugata, cleansing. I cut you. Use razor." To demonstrate, she slashes her hand to and fro, miming the shallow cuts to draw blood from Xolile's arms. "You bleed. It is a good thing."

A tremor of fear runs through Xolile, and a moth flutters in like a scrap of silk from the night.

"I'll try the snuff. How much?" Xolile asks, holding up the box.

"Give me what you want."

Xolile peers out at the black dome of sky, hands the sangoma two one-hundred-rand notes, slides the box into her bag. She slips on her sandals, then quietly moves from the rondavel. The half-moon shimmers on motionless grasses either side of the path. Disoriented, she looks around wildly, barely able to find her way to the car.

On the return drive to Mbabane, she feels stripped of protective layers; undressed. Exposed.

Exhausted, she pulls into Pine View Flats' car park. With bowed shoulders, she climbs the stairs, wide-eyed in an effort to stay awake. Is that someone outside the bedsit door? She searches in her handbag for her glasses, wipes them, puts them on. But the figure, if there was one, has gone.

CHAPTER TEN

Hills vanish into clouds. The car, a drunken beast, lurches sharply to one side then the other. The chaos of blankets, pillows, sacks of vegetables, saucepans and other equipment Rachel slung into the back is crammed too tightly to move. A mongoose streaks across the track and into giant prehistoric-looking ferns. Mbabane and U.K Aid are left behind for a visit to Xolile's family home with Rachel – full of heart. Down to earth. Strong in her beliefs.

Rain must have fallen in the night. Mist slumbers above a confusion of red mud, wattle and thatch huts girdled by the crescent-shaped driveway that loops behind the cattle kraal. The settlement looks befogged and damp. Xolile is so close the hairs on Koliwe's neck stand on end.

Children swarm out from the scrub boundary. The air fizzes as they crowd the stranger. Xolile. Shrill as piccolos the children chant, "How are you? How are you? How are you?" When Rachel scowls, they scatter. Xolile savours the clashing disorder and the deep satisfaction her aunt's company brings. Rachel leads her to a breezeblock bungalow with a galvanised iron roof. The Dlamini homestead.

From the front porch the panoramic view across open country is streaked with threads of mist. A small boy wearing a monkey-fur loin cloth stands in the doorway. Two strings of beads cross his panting chest. Sand sparkles on his bare belly like glitter on a Christmas card. A pile of whining puppies with loose-fitting skin squirm at his feet. He bends over their skeletal mother to stroke her mangy, tick-bitten coat.

"Ati," Rachel says to the boy, "say hello to your new sister."

Xolile uses the back of her hand to wipe a tear from her cheek. Ati balances like a bird on one wobbly leg. Oh, to be like this little boy, woven into the country, the customs, the wild beauty. She looks down at the scabby-eared puppies. "What do they eat?"

"Cockroaches, rats, food scraps," Ati replies.

Veiled by a silvery haze, an old woman limps towards them down a path between maize fields.

Rachel says, "Xolile, this is your gogo, your grandmother."

A floral scarf conceals the woman's forehead and hair. She raises her chin. Her face has shrivelled and withered, when she smiles the skin either side of her lips puckers; crow's feet splay towards her temples. Xolile sees both herself and Rachel in the infectious grin and cloudy coal-black eyes. Rachel embraces her mother. Claw-like fingers clasp Xolile's hands. She clutches her gogo's gaunt body in young supple arms. The feeling of not living inside herself is replaced by a joyful glow and defiant pride. She strolls beside her gogo through the squelchy mire overgrown with flowers, and between plots of onions, potatoes, okra, where once there was a path. Gogo hoists her skirt from her ankles up to her calves. Xolile searches for words. None come.

Vast boulders rise skyward. Villages of mud-and-stick houses, bungalows built from concrete blocks dapple distant hills. Does her gogo know they standing on the roof of the world? Ahead lies a wildly beautiful cloud country of spectacular mountains. Slopes chequered with ancient rock formations, grey granite shelves stacked precariously high. Clusters of huts crouch in the creases of valleys. Strands of bluish smoke swirl into the air. Xolile spreads her arms. Spins up to the sun. Bridges the gap at the heart of herself.

Turning back, her gogo says, "I put you here."

The bedroom is bare, but for a mother hen herding her chicks beneath the wire mesh bed.

Cocks crow as the mists clear. The grasslands, the homestead, thatched mud huts, are bathed in gold; the dewy air grows rich with an aroma of coffee warmed over a fire. When Rachel cooks mealie-meal porridge, Xolile lights up more. Insecurities and shame evaporate with the cooler morning mountain air.

Seated on a patch of grass beneath a clear blue sky, Xolile, anticipating the party, is surrounded by bowls of sliced sweet potatoes, aubergines, platters of dried beef, a casserole of peanuts crushed with pumpkins leaves.

"The Lord has returned you to us," Rachel reinforces, "for this we make a lavish feast."

The afternoon has a festive feel until Bandile, a surly man introduced as a cousin, arrives with his wives. Bandile has small shifty eyes. There is the family likeness – the thick frame, her father's broad forehead furrowed with scar-like slashes from so many years of frowning. The silence is uncomfortable. Bandile will not approach Rachel and Xolile, they must walk up to him.

Rachel says, "Meet your cousin, Xolile. From England," with impatience painted on her face.

Bandile's eyes burrow into Xolile. He grins slyly, as if he sees through her. He strait-jackets her into his embrace. The sour air surrounding him reeks of unwashed clothes left too long in a laundry bin. He gasps into her hair, "Oh, Xolile, Xolile, my little England cousin."

Bandile's wives admire Xolile's high forehead, her thoughtful almond-shaped eyes, and address her as Sis, moving her to bursting with passion and happiness. How does she make herself understood when she can't speak siSwati? She throws back her head, laughing with the other women, laughing like animals howling.

The setting sun tickles clouds pink. There is a peculiar feeling. Like gazing at a full blue moon. Feeling warm rain. She is weightless. Her whole body lifts.

Cattle low on a far hillside where two women work together, cutting grasses for plaiting and thatching. On the near hillside, a small boy walks through the swaying sea of grass, his voice a soothing lullaby as the goats scamper in for the evening.

Rachel talks about the kings, chiefs, clans, hereditary links and the mystery of ancient places, and Koliwe senses that the old kingdom is inseparable from the people and the country. It seems too that the monarchy is transcendent – the essence of the people and the countryside – flowing through rivers carved deep into hills, stretching through the present, creating a future characterised by customary beliefs, clans and ties of blood, betrothal or marriage. And, despite the deluge of names she can neither at first remember, nor pronounce, this history seems intrinsic, invaluable. At the very heart of Swaziland. She is hit by all the glory, the sheer dips and heights and the tragedy of the place. England's sculptured curves, cities have spread grey brutalist buildings, power, wealth, oppression, inequality, poverty, disease, like a human virus. The over-populated countryside will never again seem natural compared to these valleys shrouded in ancient traditions, rituals, customs.

By twilight, the party is in full swing. Dozens of cousins flood the homestead, sweeping her up in tides of unfolding hearts and welcoming arms. There are too many names to remember. The day is spent roasting a goat and preparing dishes for the party. Tables are laden with curries, red meat stews in ancient pumpkin-shaped clay pots, blends of beans, yams, sweet potatoes. Goatskin drums thrum to the clamour of voices chanting offerings, worshiping ancestors. The stamp of dancing feet reverberates through the earth. The clap of hands. The family lean on Rachel for stability and Rachel, as handsome as ever, is in good humour, skin puckering at the sides of her eyes. Her full-length red dress makes her look like a pillar-box, striding purposefully through the dusk.

Drunk on umcombotsi, Rachel packs the family into the centre of the cattle kraal to introduce Xolile to the ancestors. Xolile seeks, then squeezes her gogo's hand. Her gogo's expressive face is shaped by struggle, her rheumy eyes watering. Their feet sink into the bed of hot cow dung and beetles. Her gogo's nose screws up; the soft eyes shimmer. Can she smell the trouble Koliwe brings?

The sky – a space as black as ever; the waning moon, yellow. A symphony of stars dangles above the dark earth. The children draw close to the flickering flames' orange-red glimmer, their flushed faces stuffed like hamsters' cheeks. Xolile's cheeks ache from grinning. Waves of emotion surge. Laughter swirls into the night, exploding like fireworks.

Sunlight strokes the homestead's roof. Xolile's toes curl into the soles of her feet. Throughout the night a comforting breeze stroked her skin. Until dawn, the women drank beer after beer, to douse emotions words cannot fill.

The bedroom goes out of focus, a blurred shape moves through the doorway as though seen through frosted glass. Thandi? The figure swivels round – Xolile – in a tattered blue dress, stands barefoot beside Thandi. Xolile reaches out a hand. Shadowy as ghosts, the girls sprint soundlessly down cattle tracks and fast fade into a valley.

Ati slumbers on a blanket on the floor. The sheet on the bed where Rachel lay has been stripped back; her shape is moulded into the mattress. Covered in sleep, Xolile stumbles to the open front door. She does not feel the tears running down her face, only grief in her chest. Outside, a squabble of birds populates the parasol of an acacia tree. Is this fragile reality to end? Will she never see her gogo again? Is she losing the surety she has never before possessed – her place in this tight and ancient family?

Rachel darts through the doorway. "Time to pack." She shoots Xolile a glance.

The sun shines through broken clouds, down hills, like a spotlight searching tiny villages.

Koliwe twists and turns in the car seat, presses her lips together tightly.

CHAPTER ELEVEN

The sultry yellow sky crackles with electricity. The Mbabane HIV clinic queue twists along the pavement. A boy swaggers past carrying a shoulder bag splitting with newspapers. She pays for a paper. More meagre and deficient reports on missing people. The police have detained Matsapha Simelane on suspicion of murder. She folds the paper in half. She should go back to the police. Unresolved questions swirl with wind-blown litter and leaves.

The black felt of Cameron's hat bobs above other heads. He is walking past Woolworth's, crossing the road to the bus station and central parking area, gazing over the sea of people like some kind of prophet. Silver lightning slashes the sulphurous sky; an acrid smell of burning wood floods the air, but even in fierce sunlight Cameron wears the scarlet neck scarf, the tail tucked into his shirt. He melts into the crowds of men in denim jeans and girls in bright-coloured tops. Koliwe pauses – a long moment of fury. Whorls of dust blow across streets, surge down alleyways. As soon as Cameron reappears, he vanishes into a gang of boys swanking through the sun's sour rays.

Darkness is falling. Stars filter through the curtain of night by the time she locates Maureen's split-level house of white brick and beech wood on Sibebe Rock's steep face.

"Welcome." Maureen warmly waves Koliwe into a dingy, dimly lit hall. She kisses both cheeks to say hello, and exclaims, "Darling, come in, you look terrible!" Yet Maureen's face is thinner, and she is darker than a shadow, guiding Koliwe beneath shabby, dust-caked chandeliers that cast a muted glow, and through to her living room.

Koliwe's feet feel weighted to the floor; her eyes shine with tears. She is thinking about the account she is to make of her circumstances, her reasons for visiting.

A valley is visible through the French windows; pine forests spread across slopes dotted with boulders. There are two Chesterfield armchairs the colour of old ivory – and a large leather suite the same hue as the dregs of red wine Maureen tips into her glass. A Golden Labrador lolls on the cream carpet, tail beating rhythmically; a mahogany bookshelf dresses a wall; piles of tattered Vogue magazines lend a musty tinge to the atmosphere.

Maureen smooths her ash-blonde hair neatly behind her ears. "Sorry about the smell, I've only just eaten." She carries a certain stylishness in her work clothes: a short green skirt and silk cream blouse with blouson sleeves. She goes to the kitchen, chucks empty wine bottles in the bin. Her strident voice penetrates through the wall and into the living room. "Lovely to see you, darling. Have a seat. Settle in."

"Thank you." Koliwe sinks into cream-coloured leather.

Maureen re-emerges, uncorks a bottle, fills two glasses. "I hope you like red," she says in a blasé tone. Then adds blithely, "My night companion's a bottle of whisky." Although Maureen says she never drinks through the day, sticky circles, the colour of maple syrup, mark the wooden surfaces, and the air is thick with a gloomy alcohol odour.

Tensing, Koliwe throws Maureen a frosted glance. "Maureen, you know Cameron well, don't you?"

"I certainly do."

"He says he's helping a girl. Gift."

"Highly unlikely," Maureen mumbles through clenched teeth. "What do you think about polygamy?" she inquires, switching on a reading light above an armchair. "I'm told it works when the man doesn't deceive his wife," she says, "or abandon one wife for another, and when the wives give each other support. I was married by civil law. Cameron took wives by Swazi law. What was I to do?"

"You and Cameron. *Married?*" Koliwe emits a bark of laughter. She stares at her hostess in disbelief.

"Divorced." Maureen sips the wine and takes small steps across the cream carpet. "Now, where have I put my glasses? I thought I saw them in the kitchen." She hitches up her tights and jiggles her slender, milky-white body, straightening her skirt in an attempt to make herself presentable. She addresses her Labrador, "You haven't seen them, have you?" The dog's tail wags listlessly at his mistress. Easing herself into her chair, her body in a state of repose, the reading light's rich glow above creates lustre on the waves of her yellow hair, shadows in the hollow carve of her cheeks. It is only now Koliwe sees how beautiful Maureen is.

The women exchange glances. Between them, an unexpected bond is stitched together with allegiances.

"Do you hate Cameron?"

"Hate?" Maureen says in surprise. "Hate's too strong a word." Silky strands of hair fall across her frowning face. "It isn't him I hate. It's what he has done. Maybe I've learned something from him," Maureen says despairingly. She refills their wine glasses, lights a cigarette, hides behind the smoke.

"What *has* he done?" Koliwe asks.

Maureen switches on another wall spotlight, before dragging the heavy drapes across the windows. Koliwe's tousled head of hair is reflcted in the window in silhouette. "Cameron's actually very rich, though not many people know." She hesitates, examining a ladder in the foot of her tights. "He doesn't talk about his money. Some of the local Swazi have realised he's loaded. Funnily enough, they rarely break into his place. Maybe they think he's weird. Eccentric. I last spoke to him at the Mountain Hotel restaurant," she continues solemnly. "He was with that very thin blonde." She twiddles the split ends of the lock of fine yellow hair she has looped about her fingers, and adds, "Sindy. You've met her?"

177

"When I moved out, Sindy moved in."

"Cameron's your manager. He has a moral duty not to prey on you."

"And not to prey on vulnerable children, either."

Maureen raises an eyebrow, plucks her cigarette lighter from the table and flicks back the silver top to toy with the dancing flame. "Cameron didn't want kids of his own, although we have two." She shows Koliwe a photograph of two boys with auburn hair, their faces scrunched into smiles, a constellation of freckles scattered over their snub noses. "Children give us insights into parts of ourselves we would otherwise deny. The innocence, simple pleasures in life." She paces back and forth. "Our children, now grown men, live in Pretoria." There is a horrible crunch as she stands on her spectacles. "Oops!" She laughs, eyes sparkling, a hand in front of her little mouth, just like a naughty girl caught in the middle of a game.

"Here, let me help." Slithering from the seat, kneeling on the carpet, Koliwe tries to straighten the frames. One lens has a thread-like crack. "There, That's better." She passes the spectacles back to Maureen, who is clutching a hand to her breast as if clinging to painful memories.

Maureen slips her spectacles back on her nose, then immediately removes them to wipe the cracked lens. Eventually, she regains her composure.

Koliwe says slowly, "Children need so much ... looking after."

"Most adults too." Maureen rises again to refill her glass. "After giving birth, I experienced a sense of loss." She pulls back one section of curtain. The black pane of glass is specked with pearls of light drizzle. "Why did you move in, then out of Cameron's place?"

Koliwe gazes across the room as though across a dark expansive ocean. "He forced me to have sex with him. Without consent."

"He raped you?"

Tears spill down Koliwe's cheeks, as thoughts replay like a loop of film, repeating scenes again and again, releasing bullet after bullet of pain. She feels her personal landscape evolving, dissolving. This was more than rape – the forcing together of cove and headland, the intrusion and fusion of body fluids – if he carried the fatal virus, this was penetration by the spear of death.

Maureen draws another cigarette from the packet on the table, lights it, pushes the packet in Koliwe's direction.

"I'm to be relocated to South Africa," Koliwe says.

A bleak expression falls upon Maureen's face, drawing down the corners of her mouth. She looks straight at Koliwe, and asks, "Why?"

"They want me out. Cameron's afraid of what I know."

"What do you know?"

"That he abuses his position. That his relationship with Gift isn't right. I suspect he's abducted other girls. Maybe Thandi. I'm determined to stay in Swaziland, but terrified no one will believe me if I report him."

"That's often the way."

"It's as though we are passing – like ships in the night."

Maureen's level of sarcasm is high. "Then give him a very wide berth."

"I have. I am. We barely speak."

"Ships in the night," Maureen says, malignant. "I'll give him ships in the night. You'd better find another job. People have already tried to bring down that parasitic man. They failed."

Koliwe, the scared-little-English-girl-lost faces Xolile, who will risk everything to find closure, to bring divided selves together. Tiredness falls upon Koliwe with surprising speed. She wipes tear-filled eyes, and experiences the familiar feeling of wanting to run away. "You know other girls have been in danger?"

"I don't know how many he's kept. He genuinely thinks he's helping them, and maybe he is. Don't build your life around him. There's badness everywhere, Koliwe. Get out while you can." Maureen tips her head back, puffs out smoke. She isn't giving anything else away.

CHAPTER TWELVE

When dawn softens the black sky, Koliwe locks the bedsit door, clutching the snuff box. Rain has cleansed the street and freshened the air. The path runs through the rubble of broken bricks, clumps of bull-daisies poking from a rubbish tip. She wades through ochre grasses silent as light upon a river. It is eerie and overwhelming, moving alone up narrow zigzag hillside tracks.

Aloe grows around rocks the colour of soot; ferns cluster near a stream that sparkles through clumps of yellow reeds and stolid aged gum. Mist blows in waves down mountains, scuds across hills.

This is the view from the bedsit window. *He is with you,* the wind murmurs, *The past follows. From inside. Holding you back. Stopping you getting where you want to go...*

Sunlight filters through the clouds. Further she walks. The snuff box lid resists; it will not unscrew easily. The first ball she selects crumbles down her dress. The next pinch balances powdery brown on her palm. Dusty strands burn up her nose. Confused, she drifts through wispy grasses infused with the smell of soil and moss. Then she is floating, hands and feet tingling. It is one of those sleepy summery days when everything looks hazy. She is on the grey stone bridge gazing at the rippling river. Swiping aside a crocheted shawl of cobwebs and creepers, twigs snipe at her hair. What at first appears as a corpse is the body-shaped trunk of a fallen tree, posited on a leafy bed, robed in brownish yellow and green foliage. Amidst a rustling montage of leaves, she faces aspects of the girl she must help. Koliwe is Gift. Thandi is Xolile, each holds a secret the other ones know. A secret like a sign pointing in the direction she must go.

Starry white flowers flank the steep path winding down the mountainside. Half-scrambling, she descends, disturbed rubble tumbling ahead. Loose scree, small stones scurry down crevasses, over precipices into wild mountain lilies. She clambers through clouds, between silver-barked trees, through rare beautiful scents, many shades of green sorrel leaves, sharp as machete blades. Lush foliage underfoot, above, a dense canopy of red fronds. Fear fades with each step. Further down, waterbuck and impala graze on a plateau. From the foothills is a panoramic view of Mbabane – modern apartment blocks, mansions, gardens, cars – lie in orderly queues on ribbons for roads, laid as neatly as a child's toy town.

Back at the bedsit, she stuffs a rucksack with clothes. The narrow alley heaves with political campaigners and protestors. Men waving wads of election leaflets teem onto Allister Miller Street. She turns the key in the ignition, yanks the gear stick back and noses the vehicle through a street seething with energy. She speeds up after turning onto the highway. Trees coat the dry hilly countryside, termite hills like mounds left by gigantic moles, goats, fast become a blur. Swerving across white lines, she passes the mountains' huge granite lichen-streaked brows, curving up, blotting out the sky. Blunders by tree-lined crevices, the weathered lines of bare-faced slopes. Past pine plantation-clad hillsides – slits of light flit through their narrow alleys, beneath a sky brushed lilac-blue.

The guard opens the gates. She parks before Cameron's kitchen door. Cautiously, the dogs sniff at the legs of her jeans.

Cameron's glare is blacker than gunpowder. "Fifteen times you rang me. Fifteen times," he says.

"Why didn't you pick up?" she cries, swelling with righteous fury. But she cannot escape the madness created in her head. She wants to kick up a fuss as impulsively as a strong gust of harmattan wind. "This time, the truth." Her eyes prickle, her nose stings; a tear trickles down her cheek.

His eyes dress her down: black eyes, black shirt, black jeans, balled fists. "You look like you're high on something."

"You're keeping Gift at your place in the mountains."

"What if I am?" a shrewd look crosses his face. "Come for a drive. Let's sort this out, talk things through. You can rake through my belongings as part of your investigation." He jangles keys in his tattered beige shorts, then swings the door back for her to enter.

Turning to go, she yells, "I'll wait here," and slings her rucksack over a shoulder.

He swivels his hat onto his head and taps the crown down, giving his face a black halo. The guard reverses the Land Rover from the garage for Cameron. Despite the risk, Xolile seats herself beside him. She is skin; bone. Determination.

For hours, they drive through open country. The sky is a halcyon blue; the air terribly hot. Trees' branches spread overhead, creating a shadowy corridor. They ride over a bumpy ridge, the Land Rover glides to a standstill and her mind clouds with fear. Everything quietens. Quietens like before a storm.

Cameron hops down from the Land Rover. "This damn truck," he says, tugging the torn backrest of the seat forward. He digs out a rusty item wrapped in a stained strip of calico, disentangles the jack from the bundle and emits a satisfied grunt. She leaves her rucksack on the back seat and rests against the bonnet while he struggles with the spare wheel; the holding nuts are solid with rust and difficult to remove. Up in the mountains fires flare, plumes of smoke rise like mist and merge into the low-lying clouds blowing across the slopes.

Scouting for damage, he crawls in the gravel on his stomach and elbows, then rolls onto his back to reach beneath the chassis. When he clambers from the vehicle's underside, dust and rust streak his hair, sweat dribbles down his forehead and reddened cheeks, and he smokes at a cigarette furiously.

"Can the truck be fixed?" she asks.

"Not here. We'll have to walk to the lodge." He settles his hat, crushing greyish curls, looks towards the steep mountain face and forges ahead and up.

Goats nibble the short grasses of the low veldt. Children play on the periphery of a compound close to the path. Women walk at a gentle pace, their babies tied in blankets snug against their backs. They pass a wattle cattle byre. Koliwe wants to turn around, but Cameron has lengthened his stride. He swings his legs over a stock fence and tramps along the path to the mountains.

The sangoma's lucid voice hisses, *Birds disappearing forecast lightning.*

The air is moist with rain. Mountain tops are crowned with gold. Birds fly in great squadrons across the sky. Small, beehive-shaped rondavels of thatched grass surrounded by reed fences sit along the dust track. Horses graze on a slow rise ahead. Hills rise before the mountains. The mountains are magnificent, dark and foreboding; the air is close and clear.

They enter a wide valley; the soft earth is ready for planting early crops. "This valley has been cultivated for the production of sorghum, maize and grazing cattle," he says automatically. The horses stop grazing and lift their heads.

She struggles to keep up. "Maize," she says breathlessly, "Swaziland's staple. Does the country produce enough?"

"Most of it comes from South Africa."

Their conversation feels out of place. Walking silently, he quickens his pace. The path crosses the shingle of a dry creek bed. Sinking into sand, she stumbles, scrambling where grass dwindles to gravel. Little lizards live amongst the rocks; intricately flecked gold and green, they slide in and out of tiny crevices.

Climbing gets harder in dizzying heat. Her chest is pounding. She scurries on all fours, her toes slipping on her sandals' leather soles. Advancing towards the summit, she longs for Oxfordshire's rolling countryside – spongy wet grass that sparkles dewy-green. Cold, cobalt blue skies; leaves fluttering emerald-green; meadows lush with gurgling brooks, running from springs unseen.

Cameron points to a wooded patch far below. "See, Milwane wildlife sanctuary. You'll find hippo, giraffe, wildebeest. Milwane means little fire, that's what happens, flames leap up when lightning strikes the granite rocks."

"There's going to be a storm?"

"Definitely." His words are confetti blowing away, "We'll take the direct route through the river."

The sun has long passed its height. Grey clouds threaten rain. The temperature has dropped. Dark shadows fall between the rocks. Then blue-white lightning slits a sullen band of low cloud.

Descending the mountainside, Cameron bounds across a shallow creek; when he looks back, his face, like the clouds, gleams platinum-grey. And the whole countryside seems to close in as the wind strengthens. Lightning strikes the ground like forked serpents' tongues. An unearthly thunderclap ripples through her body. The tepid tingle of rain is at first a light shower. There is a pungent odour of grass and leaves, the earthy aroma of goat. A bird, carried by the wind, soars above her head, and she turns from the frenzy of sunlight to shield herself from now fast-falling rain.

She bolts onto the riverside path, stomps through damp grass strewn with snapping twigs. Water falls over rocks, grains of quartz sparkle underwater in the sun. Cameron glances back, the glare shifting in his eyes as reflections ripple across his face.

Stones skid under her squelching blue sandals. One catches beneath her insole, cutting the ball of her foot. Struggling to keep up, she wades through beds of rushes, the air roaring with water. The wind wails: *Rain. Fire. Lightning. Danger.*

Dim memories of canoeing through white water with school friends in Welsh rivers flood back. Always stay with your companions, the leader had said. The notion she has submerged surfaces – that waiting at the vehicle would have been wiser, that following Cameron will prove disastrous.

She loses her footing, screams, loses her sandals in the froth. Her feet slide again. Waist-deep and shuddering, she plunges into the turbelent, relentless flow. There is a great whirring of water. She bashes her shoulder on a boulder. Waves buffet her chin, rolling into a bulge. Foam circles moil and twirl into spinning whirlpools. She is swept downriver. Emotional currents spin back once more to that Sunday – the one she'll never forget – the grandfather clock's tick-tock in time with her heartbeat. Her father's body rising. That final glimpse – his face varnished with water. She pushes the memory down, makes it sink. Swims harder against the gurgling, gulping water. Reeds thrash behind as she finally clambers the shingle beach onto the bank; her hair is clotted like kelp, the saturated jeans and shirt cling to her soaked and shaking frame.

Thunder rumbles louder than an avalanche of rocks. The sky, an orange-blue frenzy, will soon become draped in folds of darkness. Nearby, lightning strikes a tree. She reels sideways, scales the cusp of the bank, sees only a blurry haze, stumbles onto a path, into bushes. All she hears is thunder. Her voice becomes distorted when she hollers, "*Cameron!*"

"*Xolile!*" Moving up the bank, he is lit in a flash, a blur of browns, blues, greens, screened by spear-like reeds.

Cameron plods through the heavy red quag of the driveway to his lodge. She dashes behind braced against the wind, feet cold, grime between her toes. For a second, she sees Xolile, a bedraggled reflection in the windows.

Was coming here was a mistake? There is the click as he flips down a switch. The generator whirs; the verandah is doused with light.

CHAPTER THIRTEEN

The grey air inside the lodge smells moist and fusty as a catacomb. The kerosene lamp on its cast iron stand emits a yellow flare in the corner of the main room.

"Last week, some people managed to get in through a window. The guard was shirking," Cameron says. "They stole the kettle, the iron, food from the fridge. It was a bit of a sorry affair." He cocks his head towards a bureau. "There's a gun in the top drawer, over there." He uses a shirt cuff to mop water from his forehead.

She takes a shawl from the divan and wraps the material about her shoulders. There is the groan of a doorknob turning.

Koliwe tenses. "Who's that?"

"The wind."

The Tilley lamp's flame jitters, as though seeking release from its cell.

Cameron brushes water from his forearms, goes to the drinks cabinet, pours an orange juice and vodka. "Don't you want a drink, sorry?" He sets his glass down, holds the bottle out to Koliwe, pours Vodka to drink neat, then slumps into the divan.

Koliwe takes a sip. The relief is indescribable.

"Supper?" He laughs strangely, takes a pizza base from the fridge, and peels polythene from a rubbery oblong of cheese. Ignited, the oven breathes out a blue gas odour. Cameron goes to change into dry clothes.

Koliwe leans against the steel kitchen sink. It wobbles, pulling away from damp marks on the timber-clad wall.

"Have you ever tested?" she asks when he returns.

"What for?" His eyes glance non-committedly across her face.

"HIV."

"No."

"Don't you want to know?"

"We all die eventually."

"Then why the fear of lightning?"

He shrugs.

"Where's Gift?" she asks.

He acts as though he hasn't heard her. Her eyes fix on his solid physique; muscular shoulders. He slices a green tomato, sprinkles grated cheese over the pizza, slides it onto a baking tray and into the oven.

A dusky shape forms behind him in the corridor. His eyes dart nervously round the kitchen. He swigs a mouthful of vodka. The shape morphs into a small figure moving in the doorway. She has a tightly drawn face; brown stick-thin legs.

"Talk of the devil. Koliwe, here is Gift." He adds, with a benevolent air, "Sooner or later you two would've met."

The girl, handsome, brown-skinned, aged about fourteen, with tawny golden-brown eyes large and sensitive as an impala's, watches Koliwe warily. Her dress is dirty; hair dishevelled; a red shawl is draped like a hood around over head. Gift's eyes are the same as Thandi's. Koliwe stiffens, and swallows a caustic coldness. Uncomprehending, the girl returns Koliwe's look. Then clarity comes like lightning. Thandi *is* Gift. The same wide forehead; the same cheekbones, jawline; straight full lips; neat pear-shaped nose. Beneath the shawl, her hair is loosely woven in cornrow. She draws the folds of cloth further over her head, obscuring her fragile, snuff-coloured face.

Cameron says to her, "I didn't think you'd be here," in a voice so low it is barely a murmur.

Koliwe is deeply uneasy, as though she has drawn open a curtain held closed for privacy. The girl looks puzzled. She slinks back, shadow-like, against a window.

Koliwe hisses, "What's she doing here?"

Cameron smiles after the child affectionately. "Kids," he says, with an exasperated sigh.

The girl whips around, the delicate curves of her body vanish down the passageway. There is the clack of a key turning in a lock. Like mist that has cleared, she leaves nothing.

"That's Thandi," Koliwe says. "Why is Thandi here?"

"You said she needed help," Cameron answers abruptly.

"She's *living* with *you* in your lodge?"

"The rondavel." He settles opposite her at the low ebony table. His head nods forward, he rubs his face with both hands. "Why don't you stay in Mbabane? We can live together again. Forget what happened. I was drunk. No harm done."

The flush of anger spreads up her neck. Swallowing hard, she lowers herself into a canvas director's chair.

He slides the pizza from the oven, cuts it in two. Cheese strings stretch from the slices to the dinner plates.

"Does anyone else know Thandi's with you?"

Cameron combs his fingers through curls threaded with silver-grey. He adopts a professional tone, "Gift was very young when she lost her parents. After term finishes, we'll go to the river, where there's a pool, and sit and gaze. That," he says, with a slight tremor in his voice, "is my sanctuary."

Exhausted by this charade, for a moment Koliwe is silent and still. She wonders, watching him eat, can hatred be measured?

"Why does Thandi really live with you?" she asks, barely able to bite into the thin pizza crust.

"It's an exchange."

"*Exchange?*"

He caresses the stubble under his chin. His quietened tone matches the sinister chill in the air. "It's better to enable one person's life to change radically, than try to effect small change on a large social group."

The lamplight dims, dipping to nothing when the kerosene runs dry. Outside, the dying wind whispers. The rain has eased.

Cameron flips a wall switch, but no light fills the blank space. "Generator's out of fuel," he says. "Look, I'm not denying there's something between Gift and me. There's nothing wrong with giving food and shelter in return for small favours once in a while."

Koliwe reaches a hand up to her throat, shaking her head. "You're disgusting."

"Gift gains. I gain. Benefits all round."

Wrapping the shawl tightly about her shivering shoulders, Koliwe fears he can see into her heart; as wide as the river, as deep as the hills are the feelings that lie within. Revenge sears up her spine. For what he has done. To both of them. Her sight adjusts to the muffled glow of moonbeams, then her eyes stray to the bureau where he keeps the gun.

He removes the lamp's glass chimney to unscrew the burner assembly. The kerosene he pours into the base overflows across the tabletop. He mops the spillage with his sleeve, then strikes a match to light a second lamp before setting it on an elegant wrought-iron stand. As he heads for the bathroom, "Help yourself to another drink," he calls over a shoulder.

The sound of rain drumming on the roof secretes the scrape of his keys, sliding from the table to her pocket.

He blunders back into the room, almost stumbling over her feet. "You'll have to sleep over." His face is immobile, eyes heavy-lidded. "I'd better make up your bed before this medicine" – he indicates the vodka – "puts me to sleep." Swigging from the bottle, he disappears back into the corridor, reappearing minutes later, dragging a sheepskin rug. "Or you can sleep with me."

He takes a long slug at the bottle and puffs on a cigarette, as if his demons can be vanquished with nicotine and alcohol. "I'm headed for the generator." The look he gives her is a warning not to stray. "It's in a hut at the end of the garden."

The wire mesh screen creaks as he opens it. The door bangs shut behind him.

She slips to the corridor where she had seen Thandi. A bat darts past her ear faster than an arrowhead. Timidly she knocks, and says, "Thandi, you okay?" Her trembling hand tries the handle. The door is locked. She dashes to a window. Sheet lightning illuminates the entire garden, lights each flicker of feeling within her. And in this strange, denuding glare, leaves scurry over grasses, scud across the sky. Cameron careens through the carnage, heading for the lodge.

No time to waste. She flies across the room; opens each bureau drawer with a heated fury. Rakes through a jumble of rags smelling of cigarette smoke. Her fingertips touch a solid object. The revolver is lighter than expected. She has never held a gun before. How to tell if it is loaded? She slides back the safety mechanism on the silver barrel above the side plate.

The wind wails straight through the lodge. Somewhere, a door slams. Hiding the gun behind her back, she sinks into the divan. Cameron stumbles through the kitchen; his face has a lemony glow behind the tunnel of torchlight. He shakes rain from his hair, wrings sodden shirt cuffs.

"I don't like guests creeping about," he says drunkenly. "The shed's locked, I've no idea where I've put my keys." He drops onto the divan, words tumble from his mouth, "I'm not drunk. Goingtosleepitoff."

Flat on his back, he lies perfectly still. Her eyes sweep the length of his body, travelling from the grey mop of curls, across parted lips, an aquiline nose, the stubble peppering his chin, his expression quiet, composed – like a sleeping child's – not a twitch, not a flutter of eyelids. Wind and rain battle on the roof. Within minutes, the tremor of snoring cuts the air, as raw and constant as a saw slicing wood.

She takes a lamp by its wire handle, her other hand fastened to the gun, and tiptoes into the corridor.

"Hello," she whispers through the door. "Gift," she calls. "Thandi?"

191

"Who is it?" comes the answer.

"Xolile." This time the door swings open at her touch.

The narrow room has a bed at the back, draped in Nottingham lace. Hiding the gun in her back pocket, Koliwe raises the lamp to the girl's dirt-streaked face. Thandi's hands uncurl like oily-brown petals. Shades of uncertainty colour her eyes. Her upper lip glistens when she sits up.

"Come with me." Koliwe puts a finger to her own lips. "Shush," she whispers. "I've got Cameron's bakkie keys."

A long scar runs from Thandi's left wrist-bone to the forefinger and down to the end knuckle joint; her entire fingernail is missing. Tight-lipped, Koliwe scrutinises the grisly fingertip where the nail was ripped off.

"How did that happen?"

"I tried to run away," Thandi murmurs.

Koliwe's shoulders heave furiously, her heart is a dam about to burst. Placing the lamp on the floor arouses a pool of dancing moths. She looks into Thandi's hazel-flecked eyes. The hurt is visible, audible, in each rapid breath.

"Quickly," Koliwe hisses. "We're going to escape."

She tells Thandi to gather her belongings. Thandi scrabbles beneath the bed, hauls out a bundle of clothes, ties them into a shawl. Koliwe takes Thandi's hand in hers. On tiptoe, she half-drags Thandi into the corridor.

Hard surfaces collide with a thud. They both freeze. Footsteps scuffle. From the direction of the kitchen something shatters; a tinkle from a shower of glass.

"What's that?"

The far end of the corridor is more dingy than a tomb. Koliwe lifts the lamp, the light reveals the shadowy shapes of furniture.

In that instant, Cameron charges. Flickering orange flames slither eagerly behind him; smoke drifts like incense through the air. Koliwe's legs are rigid. She manages to lift the gun.

Aim. Her finger tickles the trigger. The action does not come naturally. He lunges, his knuckles land a stinging punch on the side of her nose. The deafening report of a revolver punctures the air.

Thandi, struck by a bolt of fear, cowers close to Koliwe. Koliwe is filled with a nameless terror. She is spinning backwards. The gun has skittered across the floor.

Cameron's eyes are grey and feral with fury. He yells, "What the hell?" smashing an elbow into her cheek.

She launches at his chest, screaming, "I'll kill you!"

His arm wraps steadfast about her neck. Her teeth meet salty flesh. She tastes his blood, and her own.

"Mad black bitch!" he shrieks, shrinking against the wall. He clasps his forearm; an explosion of expletives pours from his mouth. Pain plays upon his face as he rolls up a sleeve, then staggers along the corridor, trailing red droplets.

Koliwe grabs the revolver and pulls Thandi past the flames licking the broken lamp, lapping the kerosene-drenched table. Small ripples of flame dance around the table legs. A vertical stream of anger erupts and blazes in Koliwe's heart. Fire is spreading slow and treacherous, stroking the timber walls with long red fingers. Soon the kitchen will be flooded with flames and the blaze will crawl crimson along corridors.

Koliwe rushes Thandi through the screen door. The wind throws rain into the molasses black sky. The dark verandah is slashed by ferocious sheets of water. Koliwe, careful not to slip on drenched planks, drags Thandi into the storm.

Dashing through deepening mud, sticks snap underfoot. Ahead looms the skeleton of a tree. The sky is weeping. The wind tugs at branches overhead, making them creak and groan. There is a maddening flash. Koliwe slams into the tree. Sees silver. Red. Cameron's torchlight searching the garden.

The first rock he throws clouts Koliwe's thigh. Thandi shrieks as a stone clips her ankle. A third strikes Koliwe's back; a shaft of pain slices her spine. She raises her shirt, twists round. The stinging is warm and wet. Torchlight scans Thandi's face. She looks extraordinary. The light ray illuminates her expression; haunted eyes, brimming with sadness. Cameron crashes behind, catching up. The bakkie looms into sight ahead on the grassy expanse at the top of the hill.

Koliwe yanks Thandi's arm. "Get in," she shouts. "Lock the doors." She tries the key in the ignition. There is a quiet click. Frantically, she turns the key. "Shit!" she shrieks, heart pounding, rainwater and sweat streaming down her face.

Cameron's shape can be seen through the windscreen, retreating to the lodge.

"We'll stay here," Koliwe says. "Keep the doors locked."

Thandi crumples, pressing her forehead against the bakkie window, quivering; brown face pale with fright. "Where's Mr Cameron?" she asks.

"Putting out the fire."

"We should help him."

"No," Koliwe replies, "it isn't safe."

Already Thandi is climbing from the vehicle. Koliwe clambers out. One after the other they lumber down the marshy slope. The wind is sweeping the hills, trying to drive them back to the bakkie. They brave each turbulent gust, splash through enormous puddles, mirrors to the sky. Grasses, flattened by rain, lie like a silken plain. All the trees lean one way like wind-blown candles. There are no anchors in this storm. Silver lightning spears the earth. Thandi drifts as though asleep across the garden. Bashed by driving rain, cut by the raw wind, Koliwe wades towards her. Pent-up passion and disbelief swell within Koliwe.

The huge sky above the lodge glows burnt-sienna. Flames leap from windows. Wild, wind-tormented flames. Sparks shoot from timbers, cascading down like slow-falling snow, while the flames do their work, spreading black smoky plumes into the night, caught by the wind like a message, a warning. Thandi's eyes water, a child enraptured on bonfire night.

Blood from Cameron's punch is smeared around Koliwe's nose. Catching up with Thandi, white with fear, fiercely wiping tears, she grabs the girl's arms. "It's not safe."

Thandi shrieks, *"Go away!"*

Koliwe tries to cradle the girl's head against her breast. But Thandi pulls free. Her teary eyes are striking and rare, but instead of gratitude, they hold anger.

Together, Thandi and Koliwe reel from the coppery clouds of smoke billowing skywards, shudder at the rasping noise of split timbers falling. Cameron's yell, a solid sound, swirls with ash and embers from the roaring furnace up to the stars.

He emerges in the doorway wreathed in fiery red tongues. Behind him the fire leers and lashes crimson. His face is lit yellow-white until his shrieking shape melts into the flames.

EPILOGUE

The land mass below is faintly green as the plane descends through low cloud. Xolile slides the newspaper into the string pocket attached to the adjacent seat back. Tired and apprehensive, she looks out over the wing. The investigation into Cameron's death had been cursory. Loss of life due to a tragic accident. No questions asked.

She adjusts her seat to an upright position, fastens the seat belt and braces for touch-down.

She walks amidst a crowd of white passengers negotiating their way through immigration with a barrage of clinking bottles, and one step behind a girl with legs so pale and long she might almost be striding on stilts. A swarm of newcomers form a haphazard queue. Neither England nor Swaziland felt like home. But this is a time of hope, of new beginnings in South Africa. Xolile is carried forward in the flow, and her passport is stamped by a law enforcement officer.

Suitcases, conveyed on an endless belt, trundle into sight and are hauled off as the pack of passengers loosens to a scattering. An array of faces waits at the barrier; some people hold up names scrawled on cardboard. She walks taller, can look people in the eye. Pushing a trolley loaded with cases and bags, she searches for her name. People barge by. She spots her placard and hails the driver, who shifts his overweight body towards her through the crowd.

He tips the vinyl brim of his black chauffeur cap. "Koliwe?" he asks.

"No, please call me Xolile."

He guides her across the tarmac, then hauls her luggage into the boot of a four-wheel-drive car. He has trusting eyes, a generous mouth and a cavalier swagger.

On her final day in the Swaziland office, Cameron's replacement, Terence Olatunbosun, said he was sorry she was leaving. "You are twenty-five?" His eyebrows raised in expectation.

"Twenty-three."

Terence's sleek sable skin was darker than his deep brown eyes. Hair tight-curled, close-shaved. Smooth wide forehead, cheekbones set high, a fine, flared nose. A well-groomed moustache and neat stubble beard trimmed large lips. She was impressed. At last, a black face in charge.

"You're English? From London?" He was looking at her loose hair, a mass of frizzy ringlets, gold-rimmed glasses, the caramel colour of her skin.

Later, Phepile told Xolile she had been right to get out. "Terence's here for a reason."

"What's that?"

"People say Terence had a bit of a reputation."

"Why?" Upset was etched plainly across Xolile's face.

Phepile had pursed her lips.

The taxi slows to a crawl. They are in the dusty street of a shanty town on the outskirts of Cape Town. They pass low rise dwellings of crumbling concrete, the occasional traditional thatched roof, decrepit corrugated zinc shacks, boarded shopfronts, faded grandeur, relics of a colonial past. Her attention is drawn to a girl in a ragged, charcoal-streaked dress, hair plaited painfully neat, wedged between a mattress and a mud-patched wall. The girl shifts her weight on her bare feet.

The driver stops outside a block of flats. "Your room's on the third floor," he says. He empties the car boot in humid air, heavy with jacaranda scent. The entrance is through a narrow passage. He carries her cases up badly-lit stairs and drops them inside the door. "Hei, I've brought your things," he calls down.

The engine purrs as the vehicle gently pulls away. The clatter of a bottle smashing on the pavement draws her to the window. Reflected back is a young woman behind the iron burglar bars running perpendicular to the frame; the metal is rough with rust. Her thick hair is messily drawn into an updo. The broad face, sombre; austere. Disappearing into herself she feels an irrevocable pain. Swaziland's beguiling beauty, the tragedy of poverty and disease, the rituals, seem far away.

Xolile gazes outside. All that is left of the sunset is a faint glow. A car horn penetrates the warm dusky air. Shadowy shapes shift into alleyways. Without light, the street is brooding and ominous. Within her, the deep force of the river swells.

BOOK CLUB QUESTIONS

1. How did this book expand or challenge your views on international aid and development work? Do you feel it is possible for Western aid organisations to have a profound and/or positive impact of the lives of people in developing countries?

2. In what ways did the aid organization for whom Koliwe/Xolile works fail to truly serve the local community? Where could they have made different choices?

3. How does this text present the disparities between the foreign aid workers and officials, and the people local to Mbabane? Were there any moments of true connection or understanding?

4. How do the Western aid workers, diplomats and government officials perceive the traditions and rituals of the Swazi people? Do you think this impacts, positively and/or negatively, the approach they take to development work and, if so, how?

5. Similarly, what is your perception of the rituals performed by the Dlamini family and other Swazi peoples, such as the funeral rites, Incwala and the sangoma? Why do you think they are still an important part of Southern African culture? How did they add meaning or purpose for the characters?

6. How do the themes of grief and guilt shape Koliwe/Xolile's journey? How does she navigate these difficult emotions?

7. What differences stand out to you between Koliwe and Xolile? How did the protagonist reconcile those two sides of herself?

8. What do you think is the turning point in our protagonist's understanding of her identity, ancestry and heritage? Why do you think reconnecting with her African roots is important for her?

9. From early in the narrative, an underlying mystery which haunts the text is Thandi's whereabouts. Are you surprised by what happens to Thandi? Why or why not? Looking back, what foreshadowing was there?

10. What was your first impression of Cameron? How did this change as the novel progressed and why?

11. Does the ending bring a sense of justice or resolution for you? What would have been your ideal ending for Cameron? What do you think the reality is for those like Cameron in the real world?

12. What do you envisage Koliwe/Xolile's future to be in South Africa?

13. Can insights be gained from experiencing others' suffering through reading and engaging imaginatively, i.e. can the imagination be educated through reading literature?

14. Do individuals have a moral obligation and responsibility to hear the cries of another human being?

15. How might reading help us understand the wider complex moral questions of the past, present and future – pandemics, climate change, racial, gender and economic inequalities, the agony created by war and cruelty, and the atrocities which can occur when governments and political regimes create or fail to address human suffering?

About the Author

Laura Fish is an award-winning writer of Caribbean heritage. She is a graduate of the MA in Creative Writing programme at UEA (2002) and was awarded a PhD in Creative and Critical Writing from UEA (2007).

Her third novel, Lying Perfectly Still, was S I Leeds Reader's Choice winner 2022, and came third in the S I Leeds Literary Prize 2022.

Her second novel, Strange Music (Jonathan Cape 2008; Vintage 2009, now available penguin.co.uk) was Orange Prize listed 2009; International IMPAC Dublin Literary Award nominated 2009; selected for Pearson Edexcel's Black British Writing A level reading guide 2017/18; is taught on university courses internationally. Her first novel, Flight of Black Swans (London: Duckworth 1995) received very favourable reviews in The Guardian, the Evening Standard, and Times Literary Supplement.

Since 2014, Laura has been employed at Northumbria University.

About Fly on the Wall Press

A publisher with a conscience.
Political, Sustainable, Ethical.
Publishing politically-engaged, international fiction, poetry and cross-genre anthologies on pressing issues. Founded in 2018 by founding editor, Isabelle Kenyon.

Some other publications:

The Sound of the Earth Singing to Herself by Ricky Ray

We Saw It All Happen by Julian Bishop

The Unpicking by Donna Moore

Imperfect Beginnings by Viv Fogel

These Mothers of Gods by Rachel Bower

Sin Is Due To Open In A Room Above Kitty's by Morag Anderson

Fauna by David Hartley

How To Bring Him Back by Clare HM

The Process of Poetry Edited by Rosanna McGlone

Snapshots of the Apocalypse by Katy Wimhurst

Demos Rising Edited by Isabelle Kenyon

Exposition Ladies by Helen Bowie

A Dedication to Drowning by Maeve McKenna

The House with Two Letterboxes by Janet H Swinney

Climacteric by Jo Bratten

The State of Us by Charlie Hill

The Sleepless by Liam Bell